GARVEY FEINSTEIN:
Hollywood Predator

J U L I A N   T R Y S T

Garvey Feinstein: Hollywood Predator
Copyright © 2022 by Julian Tryst

All rights reserved. No part of this publication may be reproduced, distributed, or transmitted in any form or by any means, including photocopying, recording, or other electronic or mechanical methods, without the prior written permission of the author, except in the case of brief quotations embodied in critical reviews and certain other non-commercial uses permitted by copyright law.

Tellwell Talent
www.tellwell.ca

ISBN
978-0-2288-6996-2 (Hardcover)
978-0-2288-6994-8 (Paperback)
978-0-2288-6995-5 (eBook)

Garvey Feinstein. A dreamy boy with fire in his heart.
Garvey's dreams revolved primarily around his love for the movies, and, not least, for the opposite sex. As to the fire, it was fanned partly by his natural, hormonal inclinations—testosterone, perhaps—but also by resentment, resentment for not always fitting in, for being left out of many a social setting, and for having felt like the odd one out all too often in his life.

All of that contributed to turning little boy Garvey into a highly driven man. Some of that drive ended up being spent in business endeavors as well as in other common passions in life—most notably, the movies. But another part of it manifested itself in an unusually high sex drive.

Garvey didn't always manage his high libido properly. And it often got out of hand. When he was fourteen, for instance, he would sneak his way to his neighbor's backyard, stand discreetly by her sometimes-ajar bathroom window, and peep on her while touching himself. He was caught a couple of times, was yelled at, and chased away, but still came back for more, until his father punished him, and warned him that if he ever snuck back to his neighbor's again, he would cut him off for two weeks.

Garvey loved women, but he also loved having fat pockets. His father gave him generous allowance money, which served to both meet his son's needs, but also control the often-hotheaded teenager. It was both the carrot and the stick that made sure he didn't stray too far from school and into antisocial behavior, even though said misbehavior revolved almost entirely around mischief and perversity when it came to Garvey, rather than outright delinquency. But still, whenever the boy misbehaved a little too much, he would see his allowance cut, and, by the same token, see it increase whenever he received good grades and stayed out of trouble for a sustained period.

However, that didn't stop teenage Garvey from going off the rails again with his libido, as the impulse was too powerful to be checked by a little more or less payment from Dad, especially in the absence of a proper girlfriend.

At age seventeen, the chubby, pimpled adolescent developed the habit of riding buses and the subway at rush hour. But it was less for a genuine need for transportation than for a base desire to feel up against the female passengers. He would stand right behind them or next to them and rub himself against their buttocks or their legs, sometimes with his hand. Some would pull away discreetly or give him a dark stare; some would call him on it out loud by saying, "Get away from me!" embarrassing him in front of a jam-packed subway car. In some of those latter cases, his big face would become red, as people would look down his pants and see a noticeable bulge, the hint of a tent. A remaining sizeable minority of women, however, either didn't react at all, or would actively rub themselves back against him.

That minority gave him all the hope and courage he needed to keep on doing that as regularly as twice a week at one period. But after getting loudly called out for the sixth time, when it drew enough opprobrium from the train's occupants that he had to leave, he knew it was time to stop, and that his member had rubbed against enough butts, hips, and legs, and once, bellies. Plus, taking the bus or the subway *just* to do that began to feel painfully sad and desperate, even to Garvey. He needed to stop that, especially that the school exams were coming up. So, he bought sedatives with bromide in them, hoping to decrease his drive a little. The sedatives worked, although it was hard to know whether it was mainly due to the placebo effect or the actual bromide. But Garvey didn't care so long as it delivered, and just found the name "bromide" to sound ironically like something bros would take to get even hornier.

The following year, Garvey had his first girlfriend, Maria, who was sixteen. Their relation was technically a misdemeanor in the state of New York, which made it the third type of crime Garvey had committed by that age, after Peeping Tom and Gropey Garv. But Gropey Garv genuinely didn't know he was breaking the law in this case. And if he did, he probably would not have cared given how thirsty he was for a girlfriend. At that point, he thought to himself, "Okay, great. Now, I have a girl, in real flesh and blood. She's going to feel my appetite"—which she did, every single day, and in every setting imaginable, even when she wasn't particularly desirous of it.

As Garvey started to become more sexually experienced, he realized that he had two types of appetites: One was purely physical—that is, the regular sexual excitement that gets satisfied with physical intimacy or "self-love"—and the other one was the desire for variety, for the chase and the conquest, for making a new woman his, if only for one hour. Most men had these dispositions to various degrees, but in Garvey, they seemed to be amplified.

But to make new women his, Garvey knew that, in this day and age, abducting them from the streets was pretty much off-limits, and that one couldn't do it more than once. So, he resorted to the next best thing: gaining power and influence, and exerting those to have women kneel down to him and unzip his pants.

"Have women..." Having someone do something lies somewhere between "getting" them to do it and "making" them do it, somewhere between direct force and persuasion. Garvey understood—intuitively, at least—that there was always a degree of coercion when it came to sexual matters. Yet, he didn't mind or feel guilty about it, because he also knew that the men women tended to be most attracted to also happened to be the men who had high enough status to bend them into sex. The way he saw it, women were attracted to superiors, and superiors are bound to get, have, and make other people do things for them. Hence, the blurred lines.

But Garvey wasn't interested in semantics and societal analyses of power relations. Subtlety wasn't his forte. So, regardless of whether these men "got" or "made" women lie down, the fact remained—as he once said it to his childhood friend, Peter—that "honchos get pussy."

Accordingly, Garvey set to be a honcho. He looked around him and saw who the big shots of the modern day were: people with money, people with connections, people in the higher-ups of any business or organization, politicians, and various other celebrities in any given field.

Power can be summed in any of these three phrases: "You need me more than I need you"; "I can do more damage to you than you can to me"; "you admire me more than I admire you." The more of these one has, the more power one has.

And although Garvey Feinstein never quite put it into such clear-cut formulas in his head, he still had a good gut feeling about it, as most people do. And that was the main drive behind him staying in school, especially that, as he was entering his twenties, he started realizing that he wasn't the best-looking guy in town, although his size and beastly appearance did give him some allure in the eyes of some girls. But, usually, these girls fetishized this aspect of his and focused too much on it when going out with him, as they would yell, "Oh, yes, you nasty beast!" and, "Soil me!" in intimate moments, and would ask him to grow some more body hair.

And even though there was something sexy about the contrast between a somewhat-hairy Chewbacca laying atop some pretty girl and having his way with her, "soiling" her, eventually, that made him feel as a one-trick pony, that that was his one and only draw, and that it was the only thing any of those girls would stick with him for. He took what he could get, naturally—beggars can't be choosers—but having mostly beast-diggers for girlfriends still rubbed him the wrong way. Nevertheless, when all was said and done, "taking what you can get" remained his dominant life philosophy when it came to the opposite sex.

One of the biggest challenges for Garvey was balancing his love and sex life with his other passion in life: the cinema. Garvey was a movie geek, and he would watch at least one movie per day even on his busiest periods. In his early twenties, he watched an average of 400 movies a year.

Furthermore, he was very impressionable in his youth. For instance, when he watched *Taxi Driver*, he delivered a monologue to his mom, aunt, and brother while he was driving them; he looked at the sidewalk and said, "Look at these animals who come out at night," as he pointed at a passing person who looked remotely strange. And then he turned back and said in a solemn tone, "That's why I've got to get in shape," creeping out his aunt in the process. His mother and brother just ignored him, with his mom rolling her eyes at the latest bit of her son's habitual antics.

* * * *

The following year, Garvey joined a movie club. In it, the members would watch a movie together, take notes, then gather around and discuss it. There were some girls he found cute in that club. Unfortunately for him, they weren't too interested in him.

One of the problems with Garvey was that he never knew how to be honest and genuine with his interests from the opposite sex in a way that wasn't off-putting or creepy, and how to be both straightforward and tactful about his intentions. One time, he went up to a girl at that club and asked her opinion on the movie *Casablanca*. And as she started talking, he creeped his hand behind her back and just randomly held her back with his hand while displaying an awkward smile. The girl said she had to go, left, and never talked to him again.

The only boy at the club Garvey saw was getting the right attention back was the club's president. So Garvey decided to become that. To that end, he left the club to create his own with his own limited funds. And, in the process, he called one of the neglected members from the old club:

"Hey, dude. What's up?!" Garvey enthusiastically greeted. "Listen, what do you say you get to join a movie club where you're the vice-president?"

"I say that sounds nice," Ross replied. "What kind of movie club is that?"

"One that has only two members at the moment," answered Garvey.

"Oh, I see..." a noticeably less enthusiastic Ross commented. "And do you have any ideas on how to get in new members?"

"I do," Garvey firmly replied. "Now, do you want in or not?"

"I don't know..."

"Oh, don't worry, you'll like it!" an impatient Garvey promised.

"Alright..." Ross half-heartedly responded.

Garvey wanted to set up a club in the exact image and style of the old one. Except, as a way of attracting the early birds, he scrapped fees for the first five members and lowered them for the next five. He also handed out ads that would read, "You like watching movies? How about you watch one for free on a cozy sofa, then chat about it with a group of fellow cinephiles?"

And it did work; Garvey received several calls in the few following days. Then, as soon as he got five members, he changed his ad from "for free" to "for a small fee."

The atmosphere of the new club was indeed casual, and the predominant demeanor of the members was easy-going, with them mostly laying around watching a movie while eating popcorn, before gathering up, discussing the film, then voting on it.

One thing Garvey insisted on was him being the president, the one in charge, and that he called the shots. He would often start his sentences with, "As president of this club," and then would introduce new propositions or veto others. When one of the female members—Rita—suggested a movie for the next session, he asked her to wait for him, telling her that he was interested in discussing that proposition afterwards. And once everyone left, he had her sit on one of the sofas, then took the president's armchair in the middle, and asked:

"So, what movie do you want watch next time?"

The young woman was a little uncomfortable by the whole setting, and by the way Garvey was behaving and focusing his energy on her while sporting an awkward smile. But she nonetheless answered: "Uh, I guess since we're watching classics these days, why not *Gone with the Wind*?"

"Right, right!" Garvey quipped. "Well, frankly, my dear, I don't give a damn, hehehe."

Rita saw that embarrassingly corny joke coming thirty-three miles away, but tried to laugh along anyway, out of politeness.

"You know what my favorite scene is?" Garvey continued as he moved closer to Rita. "When Rhett and his wife Scarlett were at the bottom of the staircase..." he said as he kept moving his face closer and closer to her, until he grabbed her head and kissed her. Rita let him kiss her for a couple of seconds then moved away. Garvey then pulled the back of her head to him and kissed her again. Rita struggled, but Garvey kept on going, before lifting her and dropping her on the other wider couch, and slumping down on her right after.

Twenty minutes later, Garvey was laying on the couch with Rita's head on his chest, just staring up. Garvey got up, put his pants on, and went to the bathroom, with Rita still laying on her back, watching the ceiling pensively and inexpressively.

As Garvey got out of the bathroom, Rita sat herself up, and almost timidly asked, "So... What do we do next?" referring to the two of them.

"Next, we watch *Gone with the Wind* with the entire club," answered Garvey as he buttoned his shirt. "Nice pick!"

Rita never set foot in that club again.

Feinstein loved his club, not just because of his position in it, but because he genuinely loved movies. He loved watching those stories brought to life, getting lost in the plots, identifying and empathizing with the actors' emotions and what goes on in the minds of the characters.

He would prepare a series of questions and themes for each movie and session. And after each screening, the members would make a circle with their chairs, he would stand up, and more or less recite his critique of the film. Then, he would ask the members to give their opinions and their possible counter-critiques to his, and they would have their discussion over it.

However, Garvey kept repeating phrases like, "As the president of this club," "as president," and "as the one in charge" so often that it became irritating for many, especially when he used that to invalidate the opinions of other members and to shut down counter-critiques. As a result, attendance rates began dropping and members began leaving. After a few months, he was left with half the membership, and the club eventually disbanded. Although he did manage to accumulate some money from the members' fees and beverage and popcorn consumption, as well as have another relation with another member who had some grudging liking for him.

Still, Garvey became resentful of the club's eventual failure, and never contacted or returned the calls of the former members again. But it taught him a few things about leadership—namely, that there was no such thing as absolute power, that if one gets too authoritarian with no concomitant popularity to redeem one's authoritarianism with, one would only be left with walls and empty chairs to boss around.

* * * *

A week later, Garvey was seen loitering around the NYFA film school. He was there to pick up struggling filmmakers who were feeling left out or disillusioned.

He approached a skinny young man with longish hair and a despondent look on his face who was sitting on a bench near the school, and asked if he could sit next to him. The young man nodded.

"So… Is the school open today?" Garvey asked in a not-so-smooth attempt to make conversation.

The young man looked at him for a second, then tersely answered, "Sure."

"Right, right… Oh, you're not an alumnus here! Okay, sorry," Garvey continued in an awkward attempt to move the conversation forward.

But the 24-year-old man was too consumed by his issues to have second thoughts about what this stranger wanted from him. So he answered dispassionately while staring at the ground, "I am, actually."

"Oh, yeah? Great!" said Garvey with an unattractive smile. "And so, how are things going in there?"

"Meh," answered the young man in the same blasé demeanor.

"Yeah, I know how you're feeling," commented Garvey, still in his attempt to build rapport. "A project gone wrong?"

"You know what?" said the man, looking uncomfortable but letting a polite smile nonetheless, "I'd rather not talk about that."

"Oh, come on! Is it a movie?" insisted Garvey with a foolish grin on his face.

As the young man was about to get up and leave, Garvey put his hand on his forearm as he solicited him to stay and talk to him.

"Get the fuck off of me, weirdo!" shouted the young man as he yanked his arm away from Garvey and briskly walked away.

Garvey had always had problems in his dealings with people. And that incident was a rough reminder of his poor social skills and clumsy ways that were always hovering a few inches away from the surface of any conversation involving him. A problem he couldn't seem to overcome, routinely tried to ignore, but occasionally came back and slapped him in the face as in that instance.

The main "people problem" with Garvey was that he had a hard time reading the body language and non-verbal responses of others, so he didn't always know how to adjust himself to the situation, or realize when he outwore his welcome, or when the appropriate moments to up the ante or make his move were. As a result, he often came off as an uncalibrated creep.

The dejected Garvey then got off the bench, and headed home with a bruised ego and lower sense of worth. The incident made him feel even worse in that it reminded him of another area of "people skills" he was bad at: women. He knew the two often went hand in hand, and that only added to his frustration.

And thinking back through his history did not help either, as the only times he successfully got with a member of the opposite sex who didn't fetishize him as some sort of beast was when he forced himself on her and exerted some of his club-president authority. Perhaps those were his only options.

A week later, as Garvey was strolling down Battery Place, he came across that same aloof gentleman. As soon as the student saw Garvey coming his way, he quickly turned his head away as if he said, "Oh, shit" upon learning some bad news. It wasn't the first time Garvey had gotten that kind of reaction.

As the two came closer to each other, Garvey stopped the young man:

"Hey, listen…" he said as waived his hand in a gesture to stop him. "Listen, please. There's something I'd like to tell you."

"What?" said the young man as he stopped, obviously annoyed.

"I just wanted to say I'm sorry. Sorry about last time," Garvey solemnly said.

The man looked at Garvey for a few seconds, tersely answered, "Apology accepted," then set to walk away.

"Wait! Wait!" asked Garvey as he grabbed him one more time by the forearm.

"What?!" enunciated the irritated man.

The hostile reaction looked gratuitous and incomprehensible to the still-clueless Garvey, who was a little put off by it. So he asked almost imploringly, "Why are you running away from me like that?! What did I ever do to you?"

"Because you're weird and I don't know what you want. Now, let go off me or I'll slap a restraining order on you!" virulently answered the young man as he yanked his arm away and walked away.

"I'm interested in your project!" shouted Garvey to the walking man who was six feet away from him.

The student stopped, turned around, paused, and with a puzzled countenance said, "What?"

"I am. I really am," Garvey insisted as he slowly advanced towards the wary-but-intrigued guy.

"What are you talking about? You don't even know the project I'm working on."

"But I'm getting to know the person working on it," Garvey answered. "And I know he's got potential."

The young man rolled his eyes, incredulous at the attempt of the strange, overweight man to smooth-talk him. Nonetheless, his interest was piqued. So he asked suspiciously, "What makes you say that?"

"It's because you are sad," answered Garvey. "And you have the same type of sadness that I have. One that comes from being misunderstood, from not being able to do what you're able to do because people won't give you a chance. They won't see your full potential because they're too busy focusing on superficialities about you, or some stupid faux pas. It eats you away."

The young man stood silent for a few seconds, a little impressed, then said, "Well, then…"

"Thanks."

It turned out that the key for Garvey to come off less creepy was to simply be more emotionally genuine. But it was still a fairly hard task for someone as gauche as he was.

"But I still don't know what you want!" announced the young man with a laugh denoting the absurdity of the situation.

"I just want to hear about the project you're working on," Garvey empathetically replied, feeling he was on a social streak. "You look like the kind of guy who does the kind of art that interests me. I'd just like to see what you're doing. I have money. So if your projects appeals to me, I might be able to help you bring it to life."

"Alright… But I won't give you the details, just the broad strokes," the young man notified as he tore up a piece of paper from a study notepad of his and grabbed a pen. "Give me your number and some of your credentials so I check you out. I'll call you, and we'll talk this out."

While Garvey was taking the student's number and giving his, the student continued, "And sorry if I reacted rudely to your advances," before the two men left with warm, sheepish smiles on their faces.

* * * *

Four days later, the young man called.

"Hey! It's me, the NYFA guy," he said.

"Hey… you!" answered Garvey who still didn't know the guy's name, but wasn't comfortable enough to ask. "What's up, dude?"

"It's alright, it's alright," answered the young man. "Hey, could we meet up some time this week? There's something I'd like to discuss with you."

"Sure. Uhh, how about Tuesday, 5 p.m., right at the bench of our first encounter?" proposed Garvey.

"Sounds great. I'll see you then!"

"See ya!"

Tuesday, 5 p.m. The two men arrived at the same moment to that old spot. They smiled reservedly to each other, shook hands, and sat down.

After a minute of small talk where they both asked each other's names, and a moment of silence, Garvey got to the matter: "So, care to tell me what you're working on?"

Dorian took a deep breath, then began explaining.

"It's a short film about a teenager who used to get bullied in school," he said. "So he vowed to get ahead in life, perhaps make a lot of money. Then, once he acquires a high enough status, he'd come back and get back at the guys who bullied him, or at least at guys who remind him of the guys who bullied him."

"Sounds great," remarked Garvey.

"It sounds great to me, too. But many of the producers and tutors at the Academy didn't like it—they thought it was too mean-spirited, too petty, and said that few people would sympathize with such a protagonist."

"I totally see where the protagonist's coming from," Garvey countered.

"You do?"

"Yeah! A lot of the bullying that goes in people's childhood and teen years goes unpunished. And you're basically saying, 'Fuck you!' to that rotten part of the culture that just accepts that as the norm. It's not normal, and it should be retaliated against, if only at some later phase in life."

"Exactly!" exclaimed the young man.

The two men just stared at each other endearingly for a short moment. Then Garvey broke out of it, and, with more tempered enthusiasm asked, "What do you say we get this thing started, then? No offense, but screw the NYFA. Do you really need them?"

"Not really," Dorian replied. "I went there to sharpen my filmmaking skills, and also to possibly come in contact with directors and producers."

"Well, uh…"

"Dorian."

"…Dorian! You've just entered in contact with one," quipped Garvey with half a smile.

The young man smiled back.

Garvey then instructed him to keep on working on his screenplay, send him a quarter of it once he was done, and then the would-be producer would take it from there. Garvey assured Dorian assured him he knew all the right editors and location managers to get the project going, and the young man responded with a genuinely happy and excited smile and a nod, and said, "Thank you."

* * * *

Three weeks later, Garvey had read the script he was sent, gotten in contact with a manager, and advised Dorian to start picking actors and actresses partly from acquaintances from his former Academy, and partly through ads. Dorian was more excited than ever about that project, which he thought could be his big break, or small—it didn't matter; it was a start.

By the end of that week, the two men agreed to meet and talk about the advancement of their project. Dorian arrived on time, but Garvey didn't. Dorian waited five, ten, fifteen minutes, then called Garvey. Nobody picked up. He rang again five minutes later—nothing. Dorian waited another five minutes, then went back home downhearted, and confused, not knowing what to think.

The aspiring filmmaker spent the following week trying to contact Garvey. He didn't even know his last name so he couldn't know where else to look. Eventually, he gave up, crestfallen.

"The bastard ghosted me," Dorian concluded, dejected, angry, and confused. "Or could it be that something bad just happened to him?"

Once again, Dorian didn't know what to think. But he knew he had to move on.

* * * *

A week earlier, Garvey had heard of a Spanish-born would-be director named Pedro Almóndolar when he was talking with a producer and project manager called Rick about Dorian's project. Rick mentioned in a conversation that he was about to work with a Spanish man on a project whose storyline involved rape. At first, Rick thought Pedro wanted to paint the incident as tragic and then perhaps denounce it throughout the message of the film. Except the depiction desired by the would-be writer and director turned out to be a little too lighthearted and almost celebratory for the producer's taste.

"And then we ended up talking about other projects and stories he had in mind," Rick imparted. "And it turned out, all of them had rape in them. The guy's just obsessed with rape. And he talked about it almost with desire, as if he wanted to live it vicariously through them. And I didn't want any part of that."

"I do," Garvey thought to himself. Before responding out loud to Rick, "Yeah… Weirdos everywhere, right?! Is this guy still in America?"

"I don't know. Probably, yeah," answered Rick. "Why?"

"He should go back to Spain, that's all I'm saying!" said Garvey whose interest in Pedro was intensely piqued.

Once he returned home after that conversation, the first thing Garvey went to was his computer to search for the Hispanic moviemaker. He avidly read whatever little information was available about him, then decided to send him the following email:

"Hello Mr. Almondolar,

I am a project manager and producer from New York. And I am interested in your artistic projects—namely, the films discussed with Mr. Rick Fowley. If you're still in the US, and are still interested to pursue this project, please let me know at this email address.

Yours,
Garvey Feinstein"

Garvey was both emotionally and sexually excited as he wrote that email. He was excited at the prospect of a new project, and aroused at the thought of discussing coerced sex scenes with the budding director.

The thought of having his way with a woman had always been incredibly appealing to Garvey, both on a sexual and on a psychological level, as ashamed of that as he was at times. Psychologically, it was a way out of his romantic frustrations—a woman you force yourself on could neither rebuff nor ignore you.

"Ignore me now," he would sometimes utter out of the blue when he was all by himself, seemingly deep into his musings, while sputtering a bizarrely spasmodic laugh.

Garvey was caught more than once talking to himself. But the people around him didn't think much of it, and the content of his solo utterances was never well-heard and understood by his family and acquaintances, so they just chalked it up to it being one of his quirks.

His youthful desires of gaining power to obtain the sex he wanted all but came back rushing to him at the thought of working with the director. He began philosophizing again in his spare time about the issue. A less intense, more legal way he thought of to achieve a similar effect was simply to gain societal and economic power: "You want this job or promotion? Put out. You want to have this nice upper-middle-class life with kids in that great house? Put out. You want to get access to such or such place? Put out."

Garvey periodically consulted forums on rape fantasies because he found comfort in the idea that many women seemed to share his desires, at least erotically. He didn't actively participate in the forums, because even someone as ungraceful as he was suspected voicing such desires might not be as well received, and that it was more socially acceptable to express one's desire to be victim of a crime than to be the perpetrator of it, even though both have the potential of sounding equally disturbing.

He would spend hours on those forums reading discussions and confessions of those desires while breathing heavily and with his mouth slightly agape, which was often his default facial resting position. Some passages were particularly arousing to him. For instance, in the middle of one of the discussions, one of the posters would say, "I'm pretty sure every single female has had those, whether she admits it or not." That particular sentence gave him a powerful erection and a rush of sexual excitement, so much so that he briskly stood up, took down him pants, and began masturbating to it frantically, as he kept reading that sentence over and over again.

The thought that every single woman out there was a secret sexual prey in waiting made him feel like a child in a candy store, and an increasingly powerful one at that. Another one that gave him a similar effect was found in manospheric forums, a comment that said, "Make no mistake, coercion is the cornerstone of female sexuality and female arousal."

Many men have people doing it on tape for pornography; Garvey Feinstein had two rape-related sentences.

He eventually couldn't take the passive lurking any longer, and decided to assume a female-sounding pseudonym and sign up to that forum. In the "About Me" space, he wrote: "I enjoy forceful intercourse, and men rubbing themselves against me on public transportation. But I keep it to myself… except here…"

Under *VelvetEglantine24*, he started a new thread titled, "Here's My Dirtiest Fantasy… What's Yours?" in which he told a short story about some physically big gentleman at a movie club having his way with him/her. *VelvetEglantine24* wrote:

"We remain alone in the club after one of our movie discussion sessions. He tells me to stay there because he wants to discuss the next film. I'm apprehensive, but I do, because I do have a movie in mind I want to discuss.

So I'm sitting on the sofa. He comes over, and hands me a drink. I take it, and ask him, 'So what movie do you want us to discuss?'

'What about Gone with the Wind*?' he answers.*

I say, 'Okay. What do you think of it?'

He says, 'I like that scene where Rhett takes his wife Scarlett up to his room.'

I feel a little uncomfortable, because I know how that scene plays out. But at the same time, I'm also strangely and incredibly turned on by that thought. (Yes, I get turned on by the thought of being turned on about rape! Lol [emoji that winks and sticks out tongue])"

Garvey let out a laugh as he wrote that, and said, "Haha, you dirty fucker!" to himself.

VelvetEglantine24 continued:

"He then grabs me with force, pins me down the couch. And as I try to wriggle myself out of it, he slaps me once. The slap is hurtful, humiliating, and makes me feel like sh!t. I stop wiggling for a while out of fear and intimidation. But then I resume, and he slaps me a second time without hesitation. I stop moving again, with a tear in my eye. Then I resume struggling. He slaps me a third time, then a fourth, then a fifth, until I feel emotionally drained and empty, devoid of any force or will to resist. And so I give up.

That's when he knows his prey is ready to be devoured, and proceeds to have his way with me.

He strips me abruptly and completely. He puts his hand over my mouth, leans on me, and penetrates me. His member is as fat as he is, but moderately long. It still hurt, but he didn't care—he was just there to use me. I was his object. He kept going at it, with his hand hushing my moans of pain, and eventually, of pleasure.

After some eight minutes of frenetic copulation, he leaves a warm and heavy load inside me as he groans, then heaves. He pulls, wears his pants, then leaves, not giving me so much as a second glance.

I feel humiliated, less than human, worthless... yet satisfied, and glowing."

It took one hour and several edits for Garvey to write that. As he was done, he paused for a moment to look at what he had just written. "I'm such a fucking whore!" he thought to himself as he smiled. Garvey got turned on by his own story and by his own female character, so he started masturbating again. He basically masturbated to himself, or rather to his both selves/characters, while alternating utterances like, "You dirty animal!" and "I'm such a whore!"

* * * *

Two days later, Garvey received the following reply from Almóndolar:
"Hello Mr. Feinstein,

I thank you for your interest. I am indeed working on a project right now. However, I am in the West Coast, and will only be staying in the US for a month if I can't get a project going. So it will be difficult to work on it with you unless you intend on moving here shortly. I am nonetheless still open to discussing it with you.

Sincerely,

Pedro Almóndolar"

The next day, Garvey responded that moving to California wasn't off the table if he were genuinely interested in a project. And, as such, he proposed a conference call with Pedro through which they would discuss the man's movie idea. And if the idea had a satisfying potential of feasibility and was interesting enough to him, Garvey promised he would move.

The day after, in the evening, the two men had their call. After somewhat awkward greetings, and some first impressions in which Garvey thought the other man's gray hair and demeanor made him look like a true artist, and in which Pedro thought Garvey was ugly, they got to the meat of the matter.

"So my next movie idea," Pedro explained in his Spanish accent, "is basically around a patient who escapes from a mental hospital, then heads to where a former neighbor of his lived, waits for her near her building, stalks her all the way up to her apartment, then, as she opens the door, forces her in, ties her up, and makes it a sort of mission of his to make her fall for him."

"Hmm..." hummed Garvey. "That's a very interesting plot."

Garvey went on to ask more questions about the storyline, and kept coming back to whether the lunatic man would force himself on the woman sexually at any point, to which Pedro replied that he most likely would.

"That's nice. Very nice," affirmed Garvey. "I truly like your idea. And chances are it would be a great hit, if anything through controversy."

"Yeah..." concurred a delighted Pedro.

After a few seconds of silence, Garvey proposed: "Here's what we're gonna do... You started working on your screenplay, right?"

"Yes, I am some twenty pages into it," Pedro replied.

"Okay, great. So here's what we'll do: You write some ten more pages, you send them to me, I'll give them a good read. And if I enjoy it as much as I did hearing your storyline, I'm moving to the West Coast so we can make this happen. What do you say?" suggested a smiling Garvey.

"Sounds great!" responded a smiling Pedro as well.

The conversation ended shortly after.

A brief moment later, Garvey's phone rang. It was Dorian. Garvey ignored it and went to the bathroom.

* * * *

Within the first couple of months of Garvey's arrival to Los Angeles, the two men agreed to work on setting up a proper film production company and finishing the screenplay, respectively, each on their side.

The shooting of the film started a month later. However, the two men often found themselves in disagreement over several parts of it; Garvey's main focus was the commerciality of the movie, and public reception, whereas Pedro's considerations were mainly artistic.

Once, in the midst of a filming session, the discussion got heated.

"I'm telling you, the public won't sympathize with the protagonist if he doesn't have any redeeming qualities!" said a loud Garvey. "When I read it, I was engrossed with him having his way with the woman—and you painted that very well—but you need to add something more virtuous than that!"

"What do you mean? And you only tell me this now?!" asked Pedro in his Spanish accent, irritated.

"Well, I just realized it, alright?! All you have shown so far is that the only reason he took that woman was his own sexual gratification. At least make it love!" proposed Garvey, just as loudly.

Pedro sighed, then said, "Let's go finish this in your office," as he pointed his head towards his office. Garvey told everyone in the studio to take a fifteen-minute break, and walked to his office with firm steps.

Once in, Pedro reinitiated the argument right away from where they left.

"The protagonist can easily be sympathized with because he's ill!" he charged while gesticulating in his typically Latin ways. "He's not doing good. He came out of a mental hospital. So he can't be held *entirely* responsible for his actions. Plus, look at how much risk he's taking just to have a shot at the woman he's attracted to, even if this attraction is mostly sexual."

"See, this is you problem," replied an increasingly aggravated Garvey. "You don't understand this country! And its broader public. You think Hector will be given a free pass by the public 'because he's ill.' Except he won't. Not for committing abduction, false imprisonment, and attempted rape. So you're gonna need some more redeeming qualities, or actions. And him being horny and wanting to shag some past acquaintance won't cut it! Even if he goes to great lengths to do it.

"As to that whole 'he can't be held wholly responsible...' First, we already established he was getting better and was almost healed. Second, that kind of 'it's society's fault' type of thinking, isn't as well-received in America, especially Flyover America. It may be in your socialist Europe. But not here. Or less so. *He*'ll be to blame! He'll be the bad guy. And third, the American public doesn't see lust in and of itself as a good thing. His carnal desire for that woman of his... far from being a redeeming feature, it'll make 'em hate the guy even more!

"So, for the last time, change the fucking thing! Or add something to it. Add love to it!"

"Why do you keep insisting on love?" countered Pedro right away in the increasingly tense back-and-forth. "What do *you* know about love?! You were all excited about this very storyline at first, and now you want to change it!"

"What I want and like is one thing, and what actually sells is another!" the new producer replied, before a moment of silence ensued with Garvey somberly looking away, then continuing, "And I know more about love than you'll ever do!"

"Right," retorted Pedro sarcastically. "That's why you insisted on doing the casting yourself, because you wanted to show these wannabe starlets 'love'!"

Garvey turned back to Pedro, looking both puzzled and angered by the audacity of his statement. But Pedro doubled down nonetheless, while unsuccessfully attempting to temper his incoming rant with some explaining: "That's right. You think we don't know why you insisted on doing the casting yourself? It's a small place. People hear stuff, and people talk. You think we haven't heard about the two women who came running out of your office scared because you tried... whatever it is that you tried to do to them?! About how you go around inviting random women from other studios 'for drinks'? And get turned down in the process—almost every time! Are you so desperate for pussy that you'll try to make a scene every time some girl comes to audition? We're hating this here!

"Oh, and you think I haven't noticed how your eyes light up whenever there's talk about a rape scene in the movie? And now I'm getting talk about the need to add love from the guy whose main philosophy in life is, 'My dick über alles!'"

Garvey stood there with a stony face, staring at Pedro impudently throwing at him every open secret about him for the entire month he had been there. Once Pedro was done, a heavy and deafening silence pervaded the room. Pedro Almóndolar was known for his long-winded riffs and tirades, which Garvey secretly liked about him... but not this one.

These invectives stung Garvey hard, and he knew everything Pedro crudely threw at him was true. When it came to hiring actors, Garvey did insist that there was no need for a casting director, that he could contact a number of talent agencies himself and, most importantly, audition the would-be actors all by himself. Everyone found it bizarre at first that he wouldn't allow at least the director or screenwriter to witness the trials of the would-be actors. But then, after the first few girls started running out of that room all creeped out and horrified, everyone in the studio put two plus two. These incidents quickly became a staple of watercooler talk among the staff there, but not much beyond that.

What happened was that Garvey had tried to come on to four of the women he auditioned for their respective roles. He would sit right next to them on the same couch, put his hand on their shoulder or leg. Most of the women would freeze upon feeling his touch, some would recoil, some stand up abruptly—partly because of what he was doing, and partly because of the way he was doing it: He would move his hand and himself towards them awkwardly and hesitantly, while mumbling phrases like, "That's okay... don't move... they'll hear us," "No, they won't hear us," as if he was begging the woman in question. His flustered and awkward ways were much of what creeped the women. And what made things even worse was that, most of the time, Garvey would interpret their reactions as them playing hard to get, and would double down by trying to put his arm around them. By then, all but two either explicitly told him to stop, or that they weren't comfortable, or outright left the room.

And what hurt him even more was that he was well aware, deep down, of his social inadequacy with people in general—he often didn't get along that well with coworkers and acquaintances—and with the opposite sex in particular, as was evidenced by the cold statistical fact of him being turned down by at least 80 percent of the women he would approach, despite his increasingly high status and influence in Hollywood. And having Pedro verbalize all of that for him in no uncertain terms seemed to make what he had always feared and swept under the rug an official reality—an ultimate humiliation.

Although, when it came to the actresses, at least Garvey wouldn't lock the room on them. A privilege Pedro did not get. Indeed, spurred by the rage ignited by Almóndolar's hurtful diatribe, Garvey rushed to lock the door, then grabbed the closest chair to him and threw it at Pedro, who ducked at the last second and narrowly avoided it.

"What are you doing?!" cried a clearly panicked Pedro.

"I'm responding with my own rant now!" replied Garvey angrily.

Garvey then proceeded to grab a second chair, in silence, and threw it again at Pedro, who kept backing away. Pedro dodged the second one, too, which hit and cracked a window.

"What the fuck!" Pedro cried again. "Stop! Come on! Let's talk it out!"

Garvey advanced to Pedro with brisk, aggressive steps, stood close to his face, scowling angrily at him. He grabbed his chin with his hand, and said in a hushed but harsh voice, "*You're* the talker! I'm not good at harangues. This is all I got! And that's all you're gonna get!"

As Garvey kept his face close to Pedro's, the two men gloomily stared at each other, both feeling their heavy and warm breaths on each other's faces. After a few seconds of silence, Pedro kissed Garvey on the mouth, out of the blue. This enraged Garvey even more, who then recoiled and screamed, "You disgusting faggot!" before landing a slap on Pedro's face that resonated across the room and beyond.

Garvey then grabbed Pedro by the buttocks and began groping him forcefully, and feeling up against him, as he said, "You like that, huh? Is that what you like, you homo buttfag?!"

Pedro, whose breathing got heavier, whispered a barely intelligible, "Quit it" as he was being manhandled by Garvey.

"Answer me!" screamed Garvey. But Pedro wouldn't respond. So Garvey slapped him one more time, before Pedro swiftly and firmly grabbed his hand, with his face still near Garvey's. "You hit me one more time and I won't hesitate to sink your life down the drain. I'll press charges, you'd get put away for months at best, and I'll make sure word gets out and your reputation gets sullied forever. Good luck taking off in Hollywood then. You're not big enough yet to get away with this shit, fatso. And if you ever will be, there's no such a thing as too big to fail in this business. Someone can always take you down. Always keep that mind. You do anything more to me than what you have just done, and I'll fucking sink you. You can count on that," Pedro said threateningly in the same whispery voice as his face was five inches away from Garvey's.

Garvey looked back at Pedro in silence for a few seconds, then let his hands off the gay man's body, and distanced himself a few more inches from him.

"Well, here's what *you*'ll have keep in mind: The producer... Everybody else!" declared Garvey in an attempt to keep face, as he gestured a level with his hand when he said "producer," then a lower level when he said, "everybody else." "I'm the boss around here! This is how it works. You don't like it? Get the fuck out!" he postured.

"How about this," replied Pedro with a more casual tone: "I'm staying here. And if you try and assault me one more time, in any way, I'll sink you anyway."

Garvey stood there in silence, staring blankly at Pedro, as if a part of him just died. Then, he abruptly turned around, and on his way to the door, he began yelling, "I'm the boss around here! Producer! Everyone else!" As he continued all the way to the hall, his sound was gradually fading from Pedro's perspective. "I am the Lord, thy God... Get out of Egypt... And get the frogs!"

Everyone thought Garvey had truly lost it this time, even considering the standard he had set with women constantly running out of his office. But in truth, Garvey didn't lose it; this was primarily a defensive reaction to him feeling once again powerless, a feeling he hated more than anything else, and seemed to have dedicated every waking hour of his existence to escape.

Two hours later, well after the storm had passed, and while the entire staff was left standing there not knowing whether to go home or wait for Feinstein and Almóndolar, the latter received a text from the former: "So are we adding this love element to the story or what?"

"Yes, we are. Give me a few more days to write and incorporate it," Pedro texted back.

Alone in his room, Garvey, sprawling on his couch, poured himself a second glass of rum. As he began drinking, his phone laid on the couch lit up. It was a text from Pedro. Garvey picked up his phone, read the text, then mumbled in his sonorous voice, "The hell we are! Bitch..." then threw his phone back.

After a few minutes, someone knocked on his door.

"Yeah?!" Garvey sounded, gratingly.

A woman entered and told him everyone was waiting downstairs, that they didn't know whether to wait or go home.

"Tell 'em to go home," Garvey instructed. "And tell the actors they should receive a new modified script by Friday. They'll have a couple of days to give it a read, and we'll resume everything next Monday."

"Okay, Sir," the woman answered. And as she turned around, Garvey called her.

"Hey, Helda!" he said as he sat himself up on the couch.

Helda turned around.

"Would you get over here for a second?" said Garvey as he pointed to the armchair in front of him. "There's something I'd like to talk to you about."

The woman approached cautiously, and sat on that chair.

"So..." said Garvey as he appeared to think about what to say next, or how to broach the matter. "You must've heard about a few unfortunate incidents I've had in the past few weeks. I mean those in the... auditioning period."

Garvey said the last part slowly and with an intense gaze to his assistant, as if to say, "I don't have to paint the whole picture."

The woman knowingly nodded.

"Right," he continued. "So, I want to put this under control, you follow me? These girls who come out of that room, hysterical... they can be a loose cannon."

Garvey was having a hard time getting his thoughts together because of the three drinks he had had. Nevertheless, he began pouring himself a fourth one. He offered his assistant a glass of it with his hand and facial expression, but she shook her head to decline.

"And we don't want any loose cannons, now, do we?" he rhetorically asked, to be met with another head-shaking from his assistance, this time in agreement.

"What I want you to do, Helda, is to calm that loose cannon down a bit before letting it back into the wild. You know what I'm saying?" Garvey asked.

"A little," his assistant hesitantly answered.

"See, I've come to accept that not everyone will like my business offers. And your job will be to intercept those who don't like them, and calm them down between the moment they leave my office, and the moment they leave the studio. So…" Garvey paused for a while, staring into the void. "What was I saying?"

"That I needed to intercept them and calm them down," the assistant answered.

"Right! I need to put this glass down for a while… So, yeah… In practical terms, what I want you to do is hang near that office when I'm having business with some ladies. Those who come out of it seemingly chill, casually, you let them go. You just point the exit to them and wish them a good day. However, those who come out of my office either frightened or angry, because they didn't like my business offer… You intercept those, and you tell them something like, 'Let me take you to exit, ma'am…' But don't show it to them. And instead, you circle them around the studio for a while before getting to that exit. And if they won't cool down, take them to the board, tell them to wait there a moment, till they do cool down, then you get in there and you talk to them, apologize if necessary; tell them, 'He hasn't been himself lately,' stuff like that."

The woman responded with a flat expression.

"What?" Garvey defensively asked. "Yeah, this isn't my real self. Whatever happens in there… Sometimes, you know, I come off a little too strong, but I'm usually good with people."

The assistant kept looking in silence.

"Whatever," an impatient Garvey continued. "Just… You just do that! You don't even know what happens. So, just, take them in and be nice and gentle with them, like, 'Oh, you want to have a drink,' 'I'm sorry for what may have happened,' things like that. Just… just make sure they leave the studio more calmed than when they'd left my office. Okay?"

"Okay," the resigned assistant replied. "But what if they don't? What if they leave the studio just as furious?"

"Well, then you'll have failed your job, won't you?" Garvey replied with a more stern tone and look.

The assistant didn't respond to that. Many thoughts crossed her mind, such as, "Have you tried not acting like a creep and pissing every woman off, you fat pervert?" But she kept them to herself.

The woman was dismissed, and left Garvey alone with his drinks and blurred thoughts. He was still sober enough, however, to realize that, as much as he wanted to put the onus of taking care of angry, recalcitrant women on his assistant, no assistant could be one-hundred percent full proof in making sure the disenchanted women were hushed forever. So he decided to add another layer of protection. And that additional layer of protection was him hiring another assistant.

The next day, when Garvey sobered up, he worked out the details of what the role of that other assistant would be.

He put an ad online and on newspapers, and received calls from six women and two men. He convened the women for an interview for the following day. And while, on the interview, he asked each of them a variety of questions, the criterion he chiefly had in mind was blind loyalty on the part of the would-be assistant. And he ended up picking the one who suggested the greatest potential for this characteristic through her demeanor and eagerness.

The newly hired assistant was an affable and self-effacing Indian-born 26-year-old woman named Sanjeep Raheel.

"I'll be calling you San from now on," Garvey said from the outset.

Sanjeep responded with quick nods of approval.

While Garvey's first assistant Helda's role was to pick up the pieces after her boss' failed attempts, Sanjeep's was to try and ensure the first one wouldn't have to do as much by weeding out the least desirable candidates beforehand.

"I may ask you to get some coffee, make some purchases there every once in a while," Garvey began to explain. "However, the bulk of your job will be on 'vetting' the people that come or may come to my office."

Sanjeep nodded in agreement.

What the producer truly had in mind, in plain terms, was for Sanjeep to sieve out those most likely to go along with his advances from those who wouldn't, among the auditioned and other aspiring women in the studio. And he wanted to create a new phase of the auditioning process called "pre-auditioning" where that would take place.

"As you may know," Garvey tentatively but keenly explained, "not all the women who come to audition are truly fit for what we want, for this or that particular movie. And so we usually waste a lot of time with non-starters, with women who won't cooperate. Therefore your job will be to try and weed these ones out before they even get to me. That way, I only—or, at least, mostly—get 'starters,' and the tryouts will be less problematic. You follow me?"

"I think," Sanjeep replied with a contemplative tone and stare. "But… how would I go about doing that? How do I vet these people?"

"Good question," answered her new boss. "Your first and foremost trait in these wannabe actresses that you want to look for is their eagerness. That's the keyword: Eagerness! And the second would be: agreeability, or 'malleability,' or 'submissiveness,' or however you want to call it."

Garvey went on to explain the vetting process, and the questions his new assistant would be asking in the pre-audition sessions. Among those questions, he insisted on the assistant dropping—seemingly randomly—the following: "How eager are you to get that role?" and "Would you be willing to go far to get it, or to play X?" He repeated the words "eagerness," "eager," and "compliance" so many times in his layout of Sanjeep's job description that she began to feel discomforted by the words.

Sanjeep wondered why eagerness to please and comply, among all other traits someone could want in a potential actor, was so crucial to her boss. She had her suspicions, but was too timid to ask or question that out loud. However, as she was leaving the room, she did turn around, and say rather sheepishly: "Sir, can I ask you something?"

"What?" said Garvey without looking up as he was cutting the tip of the cigar he was about to light up.

"In this whole pre-auditioning concept, you only mentioned female auditionees. Um, is there another pre-audition for males only, or is it only women that we're vetting?" Sanjeep asked cautiously.

Garvey took a long puff from his cigar, then said in a quiet but raspy voice, "Are you accusing me of discrimination?" as he let out heavy smoke.

"No, not at all!" quickly responded a somewhat flustered assistant. "I just... I just want to know why I'm doing this to the women only. That's all."

"Men tend to be more straightforward that it all shows out in the audition itself, so they need less vetting," answered Garvey in a monotonous and curt tone as he took another drag.

"Oh, okay. I get it," replied Sanjeep.

"One last thing," said Garvey in a more authoritative voice that stopped Sanjeep in her tracks as she was turning around and heading out, "I don't like it when my employees question my decisions without me asking for their input."

"I understand," an embarrassed Sanjeep said while nodding in understanding as she felt a chill in her spine at Garvey's somewhat threatening statement. She felt as if she had messed up in her first week at the job, which she was hoping would be the first stepping stone in her career in Hollywood.

"The whys and the wherefore, the macro, the meta, you leave that to me," Garvey continued. "Your job deals with the micro—the whats and the hows."

"Understood," Sanjeep reiterated sheepishly, before leaving.

A conflicted assistant left that room. A part of her resented her boss' crypto-tyrannical ways, but another part strangely enjoyed them—the part that liked the new authority under which she was now, and where her main worry would be to please said authority. She had a clear knowledge of what she was supposed to do.

The second part of Sanjeep's personality prevailed in the following weeks, if anything due to pragmatic self-interest, to Garvey's ultimate satisfaction. She felt increasingly comfortable in her role of assistant, so much so that pleasing her boss became what pleased her most. So much for the staunchly feminist Sanjeep of three months earlier, dead set on climbing the ladder of the industry, and eventually assuming the reins of a niche thereof. But humans are complex beings, and the aspect of her personality that had held sway three months earlier found itself overwhelmed by the other, more primal aspect. And even though the first part still came back to sting her every once in a while—which Sanjeep felt all too well—the intoxicating and somewhat arousing feeling of security of being under the wing of 'The Man' had prevailed more often than not.

And Garvey didn't hesitate to make the most of Sanjeep's dispositions. In addition to the usual gopher tasks of getting him coffee or shopping for neckties, and to the fishy pre-auditioning sessions, Garvey would also task the young woman of quite peculiar things. Once, after Sanjeep gave Garvey a ranking of 'Most to Least Eager' following a pre-audition—as per his request—Garvey checked the list then told her to send the two girls who topped it to the Roosevelt Hotel down Hollywood Boulevard, where he was meeting a filmmaker called Moody Alan whose upcoming project, *Broadway Ballots*, he set to produce.

Garvey told the filmmaker two of the girls he had pre-auditioned for the parts they were discussing should be coming any moment, and that they seemed fit for those roles. Their names were Ellen Chen and Evelyn West.

"Uh, excuse me… The girls you *pre*-auditioned?" asked a confused Alan.

"Yeah," responded Garvey as he was pouring himself a drink.

"What does that mean?"

"Yeah, it's a… it's a new concept. It's sort of an audition before the audition, in which I get to get a feel of who's fit for what, you know? And I had a good feeling about these two, let me tell you. And I'm sure you will, too. They're, uh, they're very eager. So I was told," said Garvey.

"So you were told? You mean you didn't even audition them yourself?" asked Moody, still perplexed.

"Listen, they're great. Ellen herself plays an actress that shouldn't have been one. So, if anything, you should be asking for *less* rigor in selecting her, not more."

Garvey drank some more, then paused, while Moody flatly stared at him as if to say, "Is this guy for real?" He then continued in a more comforting tone, "Listen, I know what I'm doing. You'll meet them, have your own feel. And if you don't like them, we'll look for others, alright?"

"Alright…" replied a still-skeptical Moody.

"Here they are," announced Garvey as he saw Sanjeep accompany the two women into the hall of the hotel.

It was the first time both Garvey and Moody saw the women. The two men had roughly the same first impression upon seeing Evelyn and Ellen; namely, "beauty" and "hottie," respectively. As the women were approaching, Garvey waived them over, and discreetly told Moody, "You stay some ten minutes tops and you scram," then stood up and greeted the would-be movie stars.

The two women looked somewhat intimidated, which Garvey took as a compliment for his high status. However, after a while, he realized their attention and glittery eyes were mostly focused on whom they seemed to see as a hot-shot filmmaker. "This is such a great honor to meet you," "I watched *all* your films!" "*Annie in the Hall*," were some of things said to the renowned Jewish director.

The two women talked to Alan about how they loved the script and initiated enthusiastic discussions with him about their possible characters with an eagerness Garvey could only dream of. Alan happily obliged and told them about the plot and the various characters. The women were hung at Moody's every word and seemed to be completely oblivious of Garvey's presence.

As a result, Garvey felt both neglected and jealous, stinging him right in his pride. He tried to soothe his insecurity by rationalizing the women's interest as them kissing up to the guy who was most likely to give them the roles of their lives. "Pff, they don't know *I'm* that guy," he thought to himself. Then he kept repeating in his head, "I am the Lord thy God" and "I'll get you out of Egypt" and such random phrases reminiscent of things a febrile patient would say. However, on the outside, Garvey was just smiling and trying to join the conversation.

Eventually, he did join the conversation by paraphrasing out loud what he was musing about.

"Hey," he interjected humorously. "I'd like to introduce the guy who'll make sure you'll be part of our esteemed filmmaker's upcoming gem." Garvey held out his hand, and the women somewhat cautiously shook it. "Listen," he continued, "what do you say we let Mr. Alan get back to his business, and we go back to ours?"

The two women looked at Garvey as if to expect more explanation from him.

"The audition?!" Garvey exclaimed.

"Oh, so we're doing them tonight?" asked Ellen, confused.

"Yeah!" answered Garvey with a kind of a dumb smile.

"But... we're not ready for it," remarked Evelyn as she let out a slight, awkward laugh.

"Ready for what?" swiftly replied Garvey. "You're not gonna split the atom. A lot of this is simply being yourself, so, be you, huh?!" Garvey went on to have that dumb laugh again, then continued, "You already won the pre-audition, so... I'm getting a drink, and I'll be back in two."

Garvey turned around and headed to the bar thinking to himself, "Smooth, Garvey. Smooth!" Little did he know that, as he was mentally congratulating himself, he left the two women feeling more creeped out than before they had met him; they, ironically, thought *he* was too eager in his approach to them, and that turned them off a little.

But Garvey was still confident, however. He leaned on the bar thinking, "I'm gonna score tonight" while grinning cockily. He pulled out his phone to text his assistant, and said, "Probably not gonna need you tonight, hehehe, but... procedure!" as he grabbed the drink the bartender had just put next to him. Garvey gave a wide smile to the barman when he said "procedure." The barman remained stone-faced, then moved on, before Garvey left a second text to his assistance: "For reals, though. Stick around the hotel for another two hours. You might do some catching."

The reason Garvey would refer to Helda as his "catcher" and to her job as doing the catching was because she was the one who "caught" the pre-auditioned women Sanjeep pitched in her direction, the disgruntled ones in particular. The way he saw it was that he was the one standing in the middle with the bat, and his job was to hit a homerun each time Pitcher Sanjeep threw one at him. He was the batter, though he wished his own bat were half as long as an actual bat.

So, as he texted his assistant, the two women grudgingly bid their goodbyes to Moody, and then looked at Garvey anxiously, apprehensive at what this pushy man was after with such a hasty, 8 p.m. audition in a hotel.

Garvey finished his drink, put the glass on the counter, then unhesitantly walked past the young women and said, "Let's go" as he headed towards the elevator. The women followed him with both a fast pace and a wary body language. As they drew near him, Evelyn asked, "Uh, where are we going?" with an attempted friendly tone.

"To audition you," Garvey replied as he was waiting for the elevator. "You want those parts, don't you?"

"We do," Evelyn swiftly replied.

Evelyn's quick and enthusiastic response had Garvey smile and think, "They *are* eager. Some good pitcher I have…"

"Well, then follow me," Garvey said out loud.

Evelyn opened her mouth, was about to say something, but then didn't, for some reason. She was both apprehensive and excited at the prospect of that audition, as bizarre as it was promising to be. Ellen looked at Evelyn with a facial expression that betrayed cluelessness.

The door of the elevator opened. Garvey stepped aside and gestured the women to get in with a smile, saying, "Please." Garvey had an inclination to indulge in excessive civilities with the women he was interested in, in an attempt to make them more comfortable. Yet, that tended to turn those women off or discomfort them more than anything else, as he often came off as needy and pushy for it, especially for someone of his status. It made the women instinctively think that something must be wrong with him to act this desperately. His "please" coupled with an inviting smile, for instance, made the both of them cringe, though they tried to keep an appreciative smile on the outside as a response.

In the elevator, all that could be heard in the tense silence was Garvey's breathing. Ellen wondered how could this man ever climb stairs if even the elevator seemed to put him out of breath. In the meantime, Garvey was attempting to discretely peak at Ellen's derrière under a rather tight skirt. Maybe that was what he was panting after.

The elevator doors opened, and Garvey laid his hand once again towards the exit saying, "Ladies first" with a smile. This, again, made the two aspiring actresses cringe and gave Ellen goosebumps.

By the time Garvey was opening his hotel room door, Ellen and Evelyn were tormented by a range of emotions that included awkwardness, fear, but also excitement at the prospect of being auditioned and possibly getting a prominent part in a Moody Alan movie. And these emotions made Garvey both attractive and repulsive in the women's eyes.

Once in the room, Garvey told them to use the bathroom if they needed to because the audition was going to commence right away. After they were done, he had them sit on the couch, and told them he would be right back.

Garvey went into the bathroom, faced the mirror, and gave himself an aggressive and challenging look, then said, "Okay, Garv. This is your chance! You're the boss. So go in there and act like a boss! You hear that? Like a boss!" as he pointed to himself in the mirror.

Meanwhile, the two women heard talk in the bathroom, but couldn't make out what was being said, except one "Egypt." They gave each other a clueless look. Ellen stood up, headed for the bottle of liquor put in a bucket on the table in front of them, and poured herself some and said, "I'm gonna need this," before taking a gulp. Evelyn just looked at her and smiled. Ellen offered to pour her some, but Evelyn declined.

As Evelyn was shaking her head to decline, the big "boss" came out of the bathroom in a grey bathrobe with thickly sewn initials that read "G. F."

Ellen almost spit her drink upon seeing this. Meanwhile, Evelyn looked at a determined-but-smiling Garvey just standing there in his bathrobe for a few seconds, then told Ellen she was having the drink after all.

"Let's start, shall we?!" exclaimed a barefooted Garvey as he rubbed his hands.

"Um, you're in a bathrobe," noted Ellen.

"Exactly!" retorted Garvey enthusiastically.

"Exactly what?" asked Ellen.

"One of you is going to play the girlfriend of a gangster, right?" said Garvey as he drew near the couch in heavy, elephant-like steps. "I, in this bathrobe, will play the gangster... Hold on, let me go get my cigar. Is there any cigar around here?"

Garvey went to look in the drawers, then picked up the phone to call room service. Meanwhile, Evelyn was mouthing to Ellen, "Let's get out." Ellen shook her head no, and made a "let's wait and see" gesture with her hand in response.

The two women couldn't talk out loud because the silence in the room was deafening, and all that could be heard were Garvey's steps and breathing.

"Hey... Hi. Could you get me a cigar? (...) Right. (...) Any type, I don't care. Oh, and where can I find the slippers? The ground is kind of cold over here. (...) Right. Okay. Thanks!" said Garvey on the phone.

As he hanged up, he turned around to the women with the same smile, and looked at them as a dish to be eaten. Or so Evelyn perceived it. As he stepped onto the ground once again, he recoiled, and said, "Oh, yeah, the slippers..." then went back to the bathroom to look for them.

That whole awkward scene was more akin to an ill-executed slapstick skit than preliminaries for sexy time—the latter being Garvey's intent. By the time a flustered and barefooted Garvey pranced back to the bathroom from the cold floor, the ladies were so thoroughly disgusted by him that the mere thought of him coming physically near them would have made them sick.

"I'm leaving," said Ellen quietly before standing up.

"What? Come on!" exclaimed Evelyn in a hushed-but-audible voice as she stood up and held Ellen. "You're not leaving me alone with him!"

"Alone to do what?" Ellen retorted. "It's obvious what he wants!"

"You don't know that. Maybe he does want to get in the gan--"

"What are you ladies muttering about?" interjected Garvey as he came out of the bathroom in brown, plushy slippers.

"Nothing," said Ellen. "We were just talking about the audition." Garvey stood silent with his mouth half-open and a blank, incredulous stare for a few seconds, before an uneasy Ellen added, "We're excited!"

"Yeah..." replied Garvey with his mouth still half-open.

The door rang. It was room service bringing him a cigar, a cigar cutter, and a lighter, all in a nice sort of saucer. Garvey thanked the bellboy, closed the door, then turned back to the ladies.

"So…" he said just before cutting his cigar and lighting it up.

As he was taking long puffs to light it, Evelyn said, "I'm scared" in a small voice and the beginning of a subtle laugh as she lowered her head.

Garvey unexpectedly heard her, and said, "Scared? What are you scared of?" before keeping his mouth slightly open again.

"I don't know," Evelyn answered. "This is all new to me. And it doesn't look like an audition?"

"Pffkhm!" Garvey snorted laughingly. "Of course it's an audition!"

Garvey became suddenly more ardent in his speech and manners to get himself in the ambience of the movie, and exclaimed assertively, "I am the gangster! I am your boss. And you are my girls. Haven't you read the script? Make room for the man!" he said as he advanced towards the couch.

The two women froze, then quickly stepped to each side of the couch. Their hearts were racing, and they didn't dare look at the excited man sitting between them except from the corner of their eyes.

Garvey settled on the couch, which he noticeably pushed down with his weight. He then extended both his arms behind each woman, holding a cigar in one hand. He comfortably sat back with a manspread and a raised chin like he owned the place, then said in a raspy voice:

"So you wanna get the role, right?"

The women felt a little intimidated vis-à-vis his suddenly more domineering demeanor, especially Evelyn.

Garvey looked at Evelyn, who answered his question with an uncomfortable nod. He then swiftly pulled his robe aside, unveiling a swollen, throbbing penis. The women froze as they looked at it. It was nothing formidable, but still big enough for the element of surprise. And Garvey began stroking it.

Five seconds into the show, Ellen suddenly got up, presumably to head for the door. Garvey immediately grabbed her forearm and yanked her back down to the couch, holding her in. Then, in a grave, commanding tone and thunderous voice, he told Evelyn to come and hold her down with him. Evelyn was taken aback by the order, flinched, and, in the heat of the moment, got up and hurriedly obliged. Garvey told her to hold Ellen by her feet as he grabbed both her hands with his over her head, while reminding Evelyn that she would get the part if she did.

As Ellen was struggling, Garvey kept looking at her mouth and her lips while he was stroking his member. He found Ellen's helplessness at that moment extremely erotic, and her sexy lips were icing on the cake. All of this amplified Garvey's arousal as he kept stroking his cock with increased ardor, while his breathing was getting heavier and louder.

While masturbating, he kept telling Ellen defiantly, "You want the part, huh?! You want the part?" Ellen nodded at first, then shook her head, then nodded again, all the while attempting to struggle herself out of Garvey and Evelyn's grip. Evelyn found herself caught up between the stick of Garvey thunderous threats and the carrot of his career promises that she obliged without blinking.

Garvey laughed at Ellen indecisiveness, and said, "Bitch doesn't even know what she wants… That's why you need Uncle Garvey. You all need Uncle Garvey to take care of you!" Then, he turned slightly to Evelyn and crassly yelled, "You hold her good!"

Garvey masturbated for twenty more seconds after that, then told Ellen to open her mouth. Ellen didn't. So Garvey told her a second time with a slap on her face, then a second slap as he repeated, "Open you fucking mouth, bitch!" Ellen did, and Garvey unloaded some three ounces of warm semen in her mouth as he groaned. He then held her mouth shut with his hand and told her to swallow; he kept bellowing, "Swallow! Swallow! Swallow!" until he saw a gulp down her throat.

Garvey let go of her mouth and of her hands. He heaved a deep sigh, wiped some of the sweat off his forehead with his forearm, then turned around a little and said, "So much for her eagerness…" apparently addressing himself. He turned his head some more and saw Evelyn still holding Ellen's feet. He laughed and told Evelyn she could let go.

The second Ellen was let go by the both of them, she stood up, picked up her bag, and stormed out of the room. As Ellen slammed the door, Garvey and Evelyn looked at each other. Evelyn was sitting on her knees on the floor, leaning on the couch, and having a vacant facial expression. She then slowly picked herself up, rearranged her clothes then her hair in front of the mirror, grabbed her bag, and left in a dramatically non-dramatic fashion.

Garvey didn't say anything—there wasn't really much to say—but he knew that was not going to be the end of it. So, as Evelyn left, he threw himself on the couch, heaved another sigh, lit up his cigar, and plunged deep into his thoughts of how he was going to deal with whatever repercussions of what had just happened. His libido got the better of him once again. And this time, he might not be able to get away with it so easily. He knew his "catcher" wouldn't be enough to handle this latest situation, and he was right.

Five minutes into his thoughts, his phone rang. It was Almóndolar.

"Pedro!" Garvey answered. "Yeah, I received your updated script. Good thing you highlighted the changes, 'cause I'd never have had the time to go through it all. (...) Yeah, yeah, it's good. Less of that socialist stuff, and more of that love. Listen, I talked to the rest of the crew, and we should be resuming the shooting on Monday, alright? (...) Cool. (...) Alright, see ya around."

Garvey hung up, stood up, and went to pour himself a drink. As he put the bottle down, he heard what sounded to be whimpers near his room, in the hall. He opened to check was what going on, and there he found Evelyn sitting on the floor crying.

"The hell is this?!" exclaimed Garvey, still in his bathrobe with his initials, with a glass and a cigar in his hands.

"Get away from me!" shrieked a wailing Evelyn.

"Let's get inside," suggested Garvey. "Let's talk this out."

"No!" yelled Evelyn loudly with tears pouring down her face.

"How about you stop making a scene over here in the hallway!" said an increasing impatient Garvey. "Just... just get in for a moment. I just want to tell you something."

Evelyn didn't respond and just kept moaning and crying, looking at the ground, and leaning her forehead on her hands. Garvey looked around the hallway, then grabbed her arm with one hand, muzzled her mouth with the other, and dragged her to his room, as she struggled and tried to let out stifled yells along the way. Garvey kept saying, "Stop!" as he dragged her, and told her he just wanted to talk.

When he got her back inside, Garvey kept his arms around Evelyn's mouth, and announced that he wouldn't let go of her until she settled down and stopped struggling. "I just want to talk to you!" Garvey reiterated. He kept his arm locked around her head and his other arm holding her body against him without saying a word until she stopped struggling after less than a minute.

"I'm gonna let go now... I'm gonna let go, and we're going to have a nice conversation, then I'll let you go home," Garvey announced. "But if you go back to struggling and yelling, I'm gonna tie you back up! You understand?!"

Evelyn abstained from responding for a few seconds, then acquiesced with her head.

"Good," Garvey said, before taking his arms off of her face and stomach. "Now, go sit in that couch," he continued.

Evelyn did, and Garvey joined her.

As soon as Garvey sat next to her, she burst out crying.

"Come on!" an irritated Garvey exclaimed. "No more crying! Listen to me..." he said as he adopted a more commiserating and intimate tone. "I know you're afraid of what might happen next, that your friend Ellen might rat you out..."

"She's not my friend, and I don't care about that!" Evelyn wept. "Even if she did, I deserve to be ratted out! I'm crying because I hate myself! Because of what I did... because of what *you* made me do!"

"Alright, you quit raising your voice on me now!" said Garvey. "I didn't make you do anything. I didn't even touch you. We had sex, and you joined in. We had a, uh, a manager trois."

A still-tearful Evelyn started laughing at Garvey's "manager," then covered her eyes with her hands, and quietly said, "You sick, ignorant weirdo."

"What's so funny?" Garvey asked, unamused.

"Nothing. Nothing..." answered Evelyn as she was wiping out her tears.

"Listen, we need to keep this Ellen situation under control," he instructed while adopting a serious demeanor. "We don't know what she'll do next. And that's what I need to know to, you know, pre-empt that."

"Okay, then… then go and find out by yourself," Evelyn responded. "Why are you telling me this?"

"Look, usually, it's my assistant who handles these kinds of things. But this one is a little more unpredictable than usual. And since you two are friends…"

"I told you we're not friends! We just met on our way here, and we had a little chat," said Evelyn.

"Okay, but you're still closer to her than I or my assistant are," an insistent Garvey noted. "Listen, I just want to know what she'll do next, alright?"

"And why would I do that for you?! You should be in jail right now!" Evelyn spat defiantly.

"You'll do it because we're in this together!" countered Garvey as he began switching his tone from pushy and supplicative to belligerent, while still talking near her face. "If I go down, you'll go down as well. Whatever crime might land me in jail, you're an accessory to it. It's a fact! And you know what else is a fact? I have enough influence and strings to pull right now to nip this one in the bud for the both of us."

"Because you are the king of Egypt?" Evelyn jested as she smiled while wiping some of her remaining tears.

"Where did you hear that?" Garvey asked, not as amused.

"When you were in the bathroom?"

Garvey stayed quiet for a few seconds, then said, "I said I would get them out of Egypt… Doesn't matter. Point is, I have juice. And I'm more able than you to get us out of this. So you're going to have to follow my lead on this one, alright?"

Evelyn looked Garvey in the eye for a moment, not truly knowing what to say to this man, then grudgingly nodded in agreement. What Garvey had just said gave her a strange feeling of security, the same as Sanjeep felt, which nudged her to go along.

First off, Garvey advised her to go see Ellen, and find out what the violated woman was intending to do. Evelyn said, "Okay, I'll go tomorrow," but Garvey insisted on her going that night. Evelyn acquiesced, but then remarked she didn't know where Ellen lived.

"Damn it," Garvey uttered. "We have to find her!"

"But how?" asked Evelyn.

Garvey remained silent for some ten seconds, then opened his mouth, but didn't say anything, and got back to thinking. "I got it!" he enthused after a brief moment of silence. "We should contact her agent!"

"But I don't know who her agent is," Evelyn noted.

"Well, we'll just look him up. It's much easier to contact an agent than an actor."

"But… how will contacting her agent is going to help us here?" asked a confused Evelyn.

"Her agent's gonna get us to her. I'll explain in the process. Just get me my laptop. It's on the bed, inside!" said a determined Garvey.

Evelyn went and got him his laptop.

Garvey then continued: "I have the names of all the agents down in the studio, but there's no time to go there. Let's first check online."

Garvey searched "ellen chen agent" and found his name in some obscure Quora thread. He then looked up the LinkedIn profile of that agent, where he found his email.

"You think he'll answer his mail right away?" asked a skeptical Evelyn.

"Maybe, maybe not," Garvey replied. "If he doesn't in an hour or so, we're going to have to go to the studio and get his number. But chances are, he'll answer. These agents are plugged in 24/7. And for a producer, they'll be available anytime, anywhere."

Garvey sent an email titled, "URGENT: Feinstein Needs to Contact Your Client" in which he asked the agent to give him a call as soon as he could. And surely enough, the agent did after twenty minutes.

"Hey, George!" greeted Garvey as he picked up. "Fine, good… Well, almost. (…) Yeah, your client was indeed there to see Alan and I for her audition. (…) Yeah, yeah, it went fine. We're not settled yet, but she has good chances of getting picked. (…) Oh, yeah? She's probably just tired.

It was a physically demanding audition… Listen, uh, the emergency is that she forgot something important. Well, I'll just let Evelyn West who's here with me explain it to you (…) Alright…"

Garvey passed the phone to Evelyn, and whispered to her, "She's not answering his calls. You tell him exactly what I told you, alright?"

Evelyn nodded, then grabbed the phone:

"Hello! (…) Yes, yes, everything's alright. It's just that, um, Ellen forgot her allergy medicine right here in the hotel. And I know that she *really* needs them, like, uh, she told me she could have serious, life-threatening fits of allergy, God forbid. And so I just wanted to drop them off to her place on my way right now. So, uh… so I just wanted to check if I got her address right. It's, uh, down in MLK boulevard, right? Oh, 112 La Brea Terrace! I was way off the mark, haha!"

Garvey wrote down the address, then, right away, headed to the other room to change. He could still hear Evelyn on the phone. "Oh, yeah, the audition went great," she said. "Fingers crossed, haha!" Garvey could hear the nervousness in Evelyn's voice. So he went back there, and gestured to her to cut the conversation short. "Okay, so, thanks a lot, George!" she said. "Good night!"

As soon as Evelyn hung, she let out a heavy sigh of relief, and put her hands on her head.

Garvey came back from the room. And as he was tightening his belt, he remarked, "I've never heard someone getting so hyper talking about allergy medicine."

"I know! I know!" Evelyn admitted, while still visibly overexcited. "I was super-panicked and afraid. It's like, I couldn't find the right energy to talk to him with!"

"There's nothing to be afraid of," reassured Garvey as he was buttoning his shirt. "We'll just go pay her a visit and see what's what."

"You mean, *I'll* go pay her a visit while you stay in the car," noted Evelyn, smiling.

"Yeah, and make sure you drop the hair-splitting when you talk to her!" Garvey noted back with the beginning of a smirk, pointing at Evelyn. "Just, you know, just tell her you're sorry, and you didn't know what you were doing. Stuff like that."

As Garvey made those suggestions, that bundle of fear and disgust grasped Evelyn all over again as the images of what had happened a half an hour ago came back to her.

"Oh, my God," said Evelyn with a countenance that was starting to betray horror. "It's true. What did *I* do?! I truly didn't know what I was doing! Here I am, all smiling, talking about this lightheartedly with you. My God…"

"No! No!" interjected Garvey as he went up to an increasingly demoralized Evelyn and grabbed her by the arms. "Don't relapse into that state again! It's not the time! It's going to be okay! We didn't do anything… Okay, it may have been wrong, but it wasn't that wrong. We just got caught up in passionate sex. It happens! You hear me? It happens!" forcefully exclaimed Garvey as he was grabbing Evelyn who was looking down. "Say it! Look at me! Say it!"

Garvey lifted her head up with his finger. Evelyn looked at him with despondent eyes.

"Say it!" reiterated Garvey.

"It happens," said Evelyn quietly.

"Say it louder!" he charged.

"It happens."

"Louder!"

"It happens!" Evelyn yelled at Garvey's face, evidently still angry at him.

"Yeah!" responded Garvey cheerfully. "Shit happens! Sometimes you have intercourse, and you get too passionate, like– like one of those BDSM! Right?! Okay… Now, on that note, let's go to Ellen's and see what she's up to!" Garvey then grabbed Evelyn again by her arms and pulled her up, saying, "Come on! Come on, let's get up! Time to get this over with!"

Evelyn's spirits were slightly up, enough to let Garvey lift her up, lean her on him, give her her purse, and push her all the way out to his car. He asked her if she had sunglasses in her purse, then asked her to wear them. All the while, the woman kept moaning as she was being dragged down to the elevator, then out the hotel, while leaning her head on Garvey, who had his arm around her. She was quietly groaning like an ill person would, saying, "What am I doing? How did I get in here?" while Garvey kept intermittently saying things like, "That's okay!" and "Come on," and warily looking around him in the foyer to see how much attention the two of them were drawing.

Once outside, Garvey opened the backseat door of his car, let Evelyn in, then got in and drove away.

Around a minute into the road, Garvey looked in the rearview mirror, and said, "You have less than ten minutes to get yourself together, alright?"

Evelyn didn't respond. Three seconds later, Garvey reiterated in a more forceful tone, "You hear me?!"

"Yes, yes…" said Evelyn as she was slowly setting herself straight, rearranging her hair, and trying to get her thoughts together.

"Here we are," said Garvey as he parked near Ellen's seven minutes later. He turned to Evelyn and said, "You have a vague idea of what you're going to tell her?"

"Umm, I'll just ask her what she's going to do now… right?" said a hesitant Evelyn.

"Right, but you're not going to just start off with that," Garvey instructed. "You also have to show that you're, like, sorry about what you did. I mean, you and I know we just got carried away—it's human—but she probably thinks it was worse than that."

"'Probably'?!" Evelyn interjected incredulously. "It *was* bad! It was horrible!"

"Listen, that's not the spirit you should go in there with!" said Garvey, raising his voice. "Are you with me or with her?"

"I'm with nobody! I don't know…" answered a disconcerted Evelyn.

"You think you're your own team? Then let me tell you something about yourself: it doesn't want to go to jail! And I'm the only person who can make that happen right now! Which makes you 'with me,' by default. Alright? We're team! Huh?!" exclaimed Garvey in a pep-talkish kind of way.

Evelyn gave a resigned nod, heaved a sigh of anxiety or excitement, then got out of the car.

She went up to Ellen's, knocked on her door, and waited for the door to open with a knot of fear in her stomach she had rarely felt before. She knocked a second time, and Ellen opened. The two women just looked at each other for a moment; Ellen with a stern, stony face, and Evelyn with the face of a woman trying to find what to say or where to begin. As Evelyn opened her mouth to say something, Ellen slapped her on the face. Evelyn put both her hands on her struck cheek and lowered her head, and Ellen slammed the door in her face.

Garvey was in the car and saw Evelyn hurrying back with a tear in her eye and a hand on her face.

"What the hell happened?! You've been there for barely half a minute!" said Garvey as soon as Evelyn got back into the car.

"She slapped me!" answered an almost-crying Evelyn. "She just slapped me! Didn't even let me talk."

Garvey turned back and mumbled, then hit his wheel in frustration.

"That's okay," he told Evelyn as he turned back to her. "She's just a little upset about what happened, trying to digest."

"I don't want her to digest it on my face!" Evelyn retorted.

"Listen, we're going back to her…" Garvey proposed.

"I'm not going back!" exclaimed Evelyn.

"Let me finish," he continued, before explaining his full plan to a nervous and wary Evelyn.

Three minutes later, Evelyn was knocking on Ellen's door again. Ellen opened with the same stern face, and said in a bitchy tone, "You want another one?"

"Please, hear me out!" implored Evelyn. "I want to explain!"

"Tell that to the jury," Ellen responded tersely and was about to shut the door again on Evelyn's face.

Before the door shut entirely, a counter-force pushed it open from outside. Next thing Ellen saw was a big man coming at her, locking her with his arm, and shutting her mouth with his hand. It all happened in the span of four seconds.

Ellen didn't get to see the man's face clearly, but she knew who he was. She was frightened nonetheless, and kept struggling, as Garvey was holding her tighter and tighter, telling her to settle down, and that he just wanted to talk to her. But Ellen kept trying to wrestle herself out of Garvey's grasp, and letting out stifled yells under his fat-but-rugged hand.

"Get that chair over here!" Garvey told Evelyn in the heat of the moment as he saw that Ellen wouldn't stop struggling.

Evelyn did. And Garvey continued, "Now, get me some duct tape!"

"What?!" Evelyn exclaimed.

"Just do it!" Garvey shouted.

A hesitant and startled Evelyn hurried to the kitchen trying to look for it, then the bathroom. In the meantime, Ellen was still trying to wrest herself from Garvey's grasp, and trying to scream, while he was holding her and telling her to stop and that he just wanted to talk.

As Evelyn was rummaging through Ellen's drawers and laundry room, she was grasped by a dizzying feeling of déjà-vu, but was too caught up with what she was doing and too induced by Garvey's threatening and unwavering commands to stop.

Three minutes later, Evelyn came back. She said she didn't find a duct tape, but found some cloth that could be torn and used instead. Garvey told her to tear up four long pieces and bring them. Evelyn did.

Garvey held up Ellen even tighter, dragged her to the chair, sat her down, held her hands, then told Evelyn to tie her wrists together.

"You're a monster!" yelled a still-struggling Ellen.

"I just wanted to talk to you. You're the one making me do this," responded Garvey calmly, before telling Evelyn, "Make the tie tight… Stronger than that!"

"And you, bitch, you're the most revolting traitor I've come across!" Ellen slung at Evelyn.

"'Traitor?'" a somewhat amused Garvey asked rhetorically. "She's the most loyal woman *I've* ever come across."

He then turned to Evelyn and said, "Okay, now, you tie each of her ankles to each leg of the chair," as he held Ellen's legs.

After Evelyn was done tying each ankle, Garvey checked back on her hands and feet to tighten them some more.

"You're what's wrong with women today and what's always been wrong with womanhood!" said Ellen to Evelyn with a contemptuous tone and countenance.

"Shut the fuck up now," casually countered Garvey right before he gagged Ellen's mouth with the last piece of cloth.

Garvey then sat down in an armchair next to her, let out a sigh, and intimately said: "Listen, Ellen. I know I wronged you. I do. And you deserve compensation for that. You must be thinking to yourself, 'He should pay for it,' right?"

Ellen nodded with an angry face.

"And I *will* pay for it…" Garvey continued, "one hundred and fifty thousand dollars. To you."

Ellen inaudibly tried to talk under her gag, so Garvey took off gag.

"I want you to pay for it by rotting in a cell for years and losing everything you've worked for!" Ellen replied with a venomous glance, before turning to Evelyn, "And you too, bitch!"

The more timid Evelyn lowered her gaze at Ellen's invective, but Garvey seemed to remain unfazed:

"That's great," he retorted casually. "But let me counter with two arguments, one pragmatic and one practical. The pragmatic one is that you'd gain more with the financial compensation than you would with throwing me in the joint. With prison, you get the satisfaction of watching me suffer a little and lose something—freedom, years of my life—but that's it. But with the money, you get both the satisfaction of seeing me lose some of my hard-earned wealth, and to some bitter, spiteful cunt, no less… *and* you get to get yourself a nice six-figure paycheck, which is pretty neat. Wouldn't that be neat?" Garvey asked Evelyn, who cautiously nodded, before turning back to Ellen and affirming again, "It would be neat."

"Still prison!" Ellen interjected defiantly.

"Let me finish, bitch," Garvey said. "Now, the practical argument is that your attempt to have me locked up will most likely fail. Not only you have no witnesses… She doesn't, does she, Eve?"

Evelyn shook her no quickly and bashfully.

"That's right," continued Garvey in an approving tone. "So, not only you'll have no witnesses, but even the potential witnesses might end up hurting you more than helping. I mean, I don't know, maybe Evelyn would note that you had a little too much to drink before the audition, that your audition didn't go well, that Evelyn's did, and you stormed out angry, and that you might have ended up jealous and spiteful as a result. A drunk, jealous, and spiteful woman might do stupid things, like make up rape stories. Right, Eve?" said a smiling Garvey.

Ellen looked at Garvey silently with frustration, then turned to Evelyn and asked admonishingly, "You'd testify in favor of this pig?"

Evelyn looked away and didn't respond.

"Answer me!"

"I'm sorry!" exclaimed Evelyn, contrite.

"If you're sorry, then don't do it! Tell the truth to the cops!" Ellen urged.

"I'm sorry!" reiterated Evelyn, who began to tear up. "I helped him! If he goes down, I go down, too! I have no other choice! Please forgive me," she continued with tears coming down her cheeks.

"Okay, okay... Enough with the drama!" Garvey interjected. "Listen, Ellen, you'll be getting your hundred and fifty thou, along with the sincere apologies from Garvey Feinstein. You get yourself something nice with them. And, of course, you'll be signing an NDA."

"An NDA?" said Ellen.

"Yeah..."

"So, basically, this is hush money you're giving me," noted Ellen.

"No, it's compensation money," clarified Garvey. "But I also have to make sure that once you're compensated, we'll leave it at that. I harmed you, I paid for it, and that's that."

Ellen sort of rolled her eyes, looked away, still looking displeased and disgusted. She seemed to have calmed down. After a moment, she said with reluctance, "Okay..."

"Great!" Garvey replied. "Untie her, Evelyn."

As Evelyn began to untie her, Garvey told Ellen she would be contacted by a lawyer about the NDA.

Garvey stood up, headed for the door, then told Evelyn, "Let's go." As Garvey opened the door, Ellen blurted, "I'll still hate you!"

Garvey paused for a second when Ellen said that, then kept moving without turning around, while gently pushing Evelyn from the back.

The two "accomplices" got into the car. And as Garvey was turning it on, he stopped, looked at Evelyn and asked, "Why are you looking at me like that?"

Evelyn looked away abruptly, and seemed to be shyly smiling.

"Nothing," she said.

"Okay..." replied Garvey, incredulous.

"I just... I liked the way you handled things back there," she continued with the same smile and furtive glances.

"You were good, too," Garvey praised condescendingly with half a smile. "You followed orders. I like that."

Garvey looked at Evelyn for a few seconds, then put his hand under her jaw, holding the lower part of her face in a sort of approving manner. This made Evelyn feel small and fuzzy, as she looked up to Garvey rather lovingly. Garvey then grabbed her with both hands and kissed her.

In the meantime, Ellen was looking out the window, waiting for the car to leave. Garvey had parked right in front of her house, and she could see both their silhouettes from the back of the car. All of a sudden, she saw the large figure of Garvey getting on top of Evelyn's on the passenger seat, and he seemed to aggressively hold her down.

"Oh, my God!" Ellen reacted.

She saw Garvey's hand lifting Evelyn's leg up. A few seconds after that, the car started shaking, violently. Moaning could be heard, which seemed to be suddenly stifled, possibly with Garvey's hand.

The shapes became blurrier, and Ellen began to perceive struggling in the car. Knowing what she knew about Garvey, she was almost certain he was forcing himself on the woman.

Back in the car, Garvey was indeed gagging Evelyn with hand, and below, hammering away into her.

"Shut up!" he said in the midst of grunts, as he was pressing his hand on her mouth to hush her increasingly loud whimpers and moans.

At one moment, it became unclear whether he was forcing himself on her, or whether her apparent struggles were just her trying to keep her balance from the forceful action.

Suddenly, the car door opened.

"Oh, my God!" Ellen yelled. "Get off her!"

Garvey heard and recognized Ellen, but wouldn't turn, and kept on giving it to Evelyn with his pants down and kissing her throat and face oafishly and passionately. Evelyn kept letting out moans. She turned to Ellen, looked her in the eye as she was moaning while being roughly penetrated and manhandled by a completely oblivious Garvey.

Ellen stood there and stared back at Evelyn for some five seconds.

"Oh, my God. Get off her," she reiterated with lesser enthusiasm this time, and rather unconvincingly, as if she were just saying things to keep standing there watching the man she hated plowing the woman she despised with reckless abandon.

Evelyn turned to Ellen a second time to look her in the eye, as her frail body was moving abruptly at each hit. There was a taunting element to her stare, and Ellen received it loud and clear.

"Look at me, bitch!" said Garvey as he slapped Evelyn back to him.

"Oh, my God. Get off her," said Ellen with an even quieter, toneless voice, and a more distracted stare.

Ellen's breathing got a little heavier. And she began to touch her belly, as if to scratch it. She put her arm against her chest with her hand on her throat, slightly twirling her body, as she was watching little Evelyn getting railed and ravaged by the beast.

Garvey kept going and Ellen kept watching and discreetly touching herself until Garvey suddenly slowed down, then stopped, and grunted, finishing in Evelyn. That's when Ellen threw in another dispassionate, "Get off her, you monster" for good measure.

"Why don't you go home, Ellen?" suggested a relieved Garvey as he was pulling up his pants while panting. "It's getting late."

"Um, why don't *you* go home?!" Ellen quipped pettily.

"Let's go," said Garvey before starting the engine, while Evelyn was getting herself up and rearranging her hair and clothes.

"Are you okay?" Ellen asked Evelyn, seemingly worried. Evelyn told her she was fine. And Ellen added, "Do you want me to call the police?!" as the car started moving away.

On their way to Evelyn's, the pair exchanged playful remarks and warm, sly looks in the car. Once they arrived to her place, and as she was about to get out of the car, she stopped, turned around, looked warmly at Garvey, and landed a peck on his cheek. Garvey grabbed her and aggressively kissed her on the mouth, holding her face and head with both hands. Right after the kiss, Evelyn fondly stared at him for a few seconds, and Garvey stared back with a satisfied look and the beginning of a smile, as if to say, "I am satisfied with how things are working out."

Evelyn got home, and Garvey drove away.

* * * *

The next day, Garvey assisted at a part of the shooting of Almóndolar's movie, and argued with the Spanish man—again—on how much say the mental patient should give the woman on what was about to happen to her.

Pedro looked exasperated at having to go through that argument with Garvey one more time. But Garvey insisted that as much as he liked the idea, the patient forcing himself as arbitrarily would look and feel too rape-like to the mainstream American audience for it to be viewed as a love story. Some of the actors and crew present raised some eyebrows upon hearing Garvey's "as much as I like that" in reference to the rape.

Five minutes later, Garvey and Pedro were back in the producer's office, seated. Pedro looked somewhat annoyed and bored. But the two men ended up having a surprisingly intellectual conversation on whether love could result from coercion or not.

Pedro argued that it certainly could, that men loved the things that they owned, and that some women did see control and possessiveness as a sign of love. Garvey replied that while he largely agreed with the premise, it still would not go down well with mainstream America.

"I'm talking to you not as a man with this or that opinion on love," Garvey stated, "but as a producer."

Pedro eventually agreed to tone it down, and the shooting resumed right afterwards.

Garvey sighed heavily in weariness as Pedro left the room, then just sat there for a moment looking distractedly into the void, until his phone vibrated.

"Can't stop thinking about last night," read the text. It was from Evelyn.

"That's why we should recreate it," Garvey wrote back. "Care to join for a stroll near Ellen's tonight?"

Two minutes later, Evelyn sent back, "LOL you're bad!"

Garvey told Evelyn he would come and pick her up later that week for a little excursion, but had her promise to keep their relation secret until "some time after the movie," referring to the movie Evelyn was about to star in.

Garvey then dropped the phone on the desk, turned to his computer, logged into his favorite forum, and clicked on a thread entitled, "Abducted by a human monster," then on a compilation of photos from a different site called, "The Rougher the Better."

Five minutes later, his assistant Helda knocked, then opened the door. She was faced with a standing Garvey with his pants down frantically jerking his cock and saying, "Oh, yeah, use that tied-up bitch!"

"Oh, Jeez!" shrieked Helda as she flinched at the sight.

As she was about to turn around, Garvey yelled, "Hold on!" Helda turned back with her hand covering her eye. "Hold on," Garvey continued while still masturbating, "Wait here, I'm almost done!"

"I can come back," replied a flustered Helda. "I'll just be..."

"I said wait here!" screamed a sweaty Garvey as he kept going.

Helda approached his desk with her hand still near her eyes, and just sat there hearing nothing but Garvey's snore-like heavy breathing and groans as he was looking at the pictures of women getting sexually used and abused in the most degrading ways.

"Lower that cut on that blouse," Garvey told his assistant.

"What?" asked a deeply distressed Helda, with her hand still above her eyes and fingers slightly apart that she could peak a few glances.

"Just do it, and let me finish!"

Helda slowly undid one button of her blouse.

"One more," ordered Garvey.

"No, please..."

"I said one more!" he thundered.

Helda undid the two remaining buttons and spread her blouse open, baring most of breasts.

"Oh, yeah!" said Garvey in a groaning voice as he kept fervently masturbating, before he grumbled in pleasure, then in relief.

"Ah..." he continued, sighing in relief. "Look at what your tits did," he said while looking at his bespattered desk.

"Fucking sluts," he commented as he took a roll of paper towel out of a drawer and began wiping.

Helda quickly buttoned up her shirt and rushed for the door with her head down.

"Hold on!" shouted Garvey. Helda stopped and turned around. "Listen, there's something I want to talk... Are you crying?"

"No," Helda replied in a quiet and dispassionate voice.

"I thought you were about to cry, heh!" noted Garvey with his typical oafish manner. "Come on, have a seat."

Helda came back in and sat down in that same armchair. Garvey said he didn't know this could upset her, before reminding Helda that it was her duty to assist him as his assistant.

"But not that kind of assistance," she remarked.

"Yes, *that* kind of assistance included!" Garvey stressed. "You're my assistant, and you'll assist me in what I want assistance with. It's, like, your job!"

Helda didn't respond, but then instead asked, "So what were you going to tell me?"

"Yes!" Garvey said enthusiastically. "What I was going to call you for... I want a lawyer," he announced as he sat on the chair next to her. "Not a hot-shot, established one, but more like up-and-coming. So you look me up the names and contact info of five of them in the area and you forward them to me."

Garvey already had two assistants dealing with the women coming in and the women coming out. But based on the last incident, he realized that some encounters might leave the auditioned girls too fired up to be handled by "The Catcher" alone. So, he figured he needed another stick, a more potent Catcher, one who might be fluent in legalese, enough to either scare or dishearten the malcontents into taking the hush money and laying low.

Later that week, he met with an energetic young lawyer named Stuart Aaronsohn, who came to Garvey's office.

"Please, have a seat," said Garvey invitingly.

"Thank you," said the lawyer as he sat down.

After some twenty seconds of small talk, Garvey cut to the chase.

"So here's the deal," Garvey prefaced. "As you may know, in the course of my job, I get many people who come in and try to be actors and actresses. And some will be willing to do anything to get ahead."

The lawyer nodded knowingly, and Garvey continued.

"And *that*... that 'them doing anything to get ahead' is bound to get some of us in the casting and production, those behind the counter– it's bound to get some of us tempted to, uh, get intimate with them…"

"Gotcha!" said the lawyer.

"Really? So, you see where I'm going with this?" Garvey asked with a raised eyebrow.

"I think I am, yes," said Stuart with a slight knowing nod and eyes half-closed.

"How did ya figure?" asked a curious Garvey while displaying his usual standard expression of elevated chin and mouth agape after he asked.

"You think you're the first man in Hollywood who called a lawyer to clean up these kinds of messes?" Stuart asked rhetorically.

"Preemptively!" remarked Garvey.

"Right," nodded the lawyer. "And that's the smart move."

Garvey felt a little fuzzy at the lawyer's compliment and tried to contain a shy smile as a result. He then pulled himself together, coughed, and continued:

"So, uh– so, I don't know about the frequency at which I'll be calling your services. But what I do know is that I'd like your services to include you convincing some person with whom I, uh, I presumably had an adverse encounter…"

"With all due respect," interjected the lawyer, "there's no need for the fancy talk. You want me to get them to keep quiet about happened, is that it?"

Garvey banged on his desk then pointed to Stuart in approval, "That's exactly it!" before looking to his left and saying, "I like this guy!" as he pointed to Stuart with his head.

Stuart looked to Garvey's left, but there wasn't anybody there, before looking back to Garvey, bemused.

"No, nothing," Garvey dismissively reassured the lawyer. "It's just something those wops I grew up with used to do. I picked it up. Anyway, so it'll be basically like this: I call you to take care of it. You come by, go to the dissatisfied person in question, and you work your magic. In short, I'd like you to make them realize that their possible attempts at lawsuiting me won't be very fruitful, and that it's in their best interest to just take the money and keep it at that, which, let's be honest, it is. You deal with the legalities of what they should and shouldn't sign."

The lawyer was about the insert a word in, but Garvey continued, "But here's the thing: I'd like you to be available enough to come by within the twelve hours. Because, you know, the matter might be urgent, and it might need dealing with right away, you follow me?"

"Right," said the lawyer in a neutral tone.

"Now, mostly, you'll have to deal with either my pitcher or my catcher, because they'll be the ones dealing with these girls, so they'll be the ones to call y--"

"Uh, excuse me," interjected Stuart with a confused look on his face. "Your 'pitcher'?"

"Right!" said Garvey as he let out a little laugh. "Yeah, my 'pitcher' assistant takes care of the people coming in, and the 'catcher' of the disgruntled elements coming out. So, yeah, I'm just referring to my assistants. And on that, I'll make sure you'll have a pleasant time with each of them. They're lovely ladies."

As Garvey said that, he began thinking of ways to make his assistants more congenial to his lawyer. "If I make them more compliant and his dealing with them more pleasant," Garvey's thinking went, "he'll be more eager to come at my call, and perhaps not charge availability fees." In sum, Garvey wanted to transfer some of the costs onto his assistants.

Garvey and Stuart ended up discussing and agreeing on the fees, before Stuart left. Garvey then laid back on his chair, put both hands over his head, let out a sigh, and thought to himself, "How am I gonna get these chicks to please this dude?" He then let a casual chuckle, then mumbled, "Obviously…"

* * * *

The day after, Garvey was having lunch at a nice restaurant with Evelyn.

"Don't worry about the role," he said reassuringly with food in his mouth. "You got it."

"What about Ellen?" Evelyn asked.

"What do you care if she got selected or not?" Garvey asked casually as he was cutting his meat.

"Um, you know why," Evelyn replied with a sassy tone and facial expression.

"She got the role and you'll be sharing the screen on many scenes," Garvey intimated in a seemingly begrudging manner.

Evelyn paused for a second to digest the information while looking at the table, then asked while sounding mildly outraged, "How come you know that and neither Alan nor my agent told me anything?"

"Because I got the money," Garvey responded curtly and in a hoarse voice, still looking bothered and disinterested by the conversation. "Why don't you go to the bathroom?" he continued, patronizingly.

"What?" asked a confounded Evelyn.

"Just go to the bathroom and do something there then come back," Garvey repeated as he looked her straight in the eye.

Evelyn looked back at him for three seconds with a somewhat confused expression, then stood up and went to the bathroom. As she was walking away, Garvey pulled out his phone and dialed a number:

"Hey, Helda. Is San around? (...) Alright, you call her in. I'll be in the studio in less than an hour."

Garvey then hung up, got up, and headed to the bathroom as well. He operated a quick visual scan around him, then opened the bathroom door. Once in, he made a sniff "smells good" expression. After which, he turned to the stalls, ducked down to check if anybody was there, one by one; there was no one in the first one, the second one was empty as well...

At that moment, a woman entered and was taken aback by the sight of a man checking under the stall doors in a ladies' room. She instantly made a step back and left before even setting two feet in the room.

Garvey thought he heard someone come in, but when he turned around, he didn't find anybody. He moved on to the third stall and found a woman sitting with her panties down. He thoughtfully looked at the floor for a second, trying to remember whether Evelyn wore those dark red shoes that day or not. He faced the floor with parted lips and an absent-minded stare for some ten seconds trying to remember Evelyn's shoes.

He then nodded and slammed the door open. Evelyn let out a high-pitched scream in fear. She had been sensing a presence behind the door a few seconds earlier, which made her heart rate accelerate, but then convinced herself that it was all in her head, only to see the door burst open and a beastly man appear.

As soon as she screeched, Garvey swiftly grabbed the back of her head with one hand and gagged her mouth with the other.

"It's me, Garv!" he announced.

But Evelyn had already gotten into a fit of attempted struggle and screaming, with her pants and panties at ankle level.

Garvey kept telling her it was him while holding her tight. At one point, he said, "Why don't you suck my dick?" because that was what he came in there for. He began trying to rub his hardening penis against her crotch as she was still struggling. When he felt his pants down there getting moist, he added, "You're getting wet, huh?"

It was actually pee. Evelyn hadn't wiped herself yet, and let out a little more when the scare began.

But Evelyn seemed to have entered a state of frenzy due to the shock, and couldn't get herself to stop if she wanted. Her subconscious brain took over, told her to panic, and she did just that, even when the conscious part sort of realized it was Garvey and that he was probably just trying to have sex with her there as some kind of exciting surprise.

But it was too exciting. All of that had been happening in a span of two minutes since Garvey got up from his chair.

Suddenly, a waiter stormed in after he was informed of the presence of a man in the women's restroom. He saw Garvey appearing to force himself on the woman trying to wrestle herself from him, but he also saw that Garvey was considerably bigger than him, so ran out of the bathroom quickly.

In the meantime, Garvey whipped out his hardening member and began to rub it against Evelyn while clumsily and ungracefully kissing her throat, and mumbling in a deep voice, "Oh, yeah… I just wanted to surprise you, baby."

Thirty seconds later, the waiter came back with a taser. By that moment, Evelyn had already begun to give in, and her breathing was getting heavier as Garvey was rubbing his cock against her and took his hand from her mouth to roughly fondle her butt. As she began to moan, Garvey said, "You're such a fucking whore…"

"Get away from her!" someone shouted behind the two of them.

Garvey turned around and said, "What? We came together! Get outta here!"

As Garvey was about to turn back to Evelyn, the waiter launched his taser which immediately paralyzed Garvey… and Evelyn, who received almost as much juice as her beau did. An unintended twofer for Dylan, the waiter.

As soon as Dylan realized that—five seconds in—he stopped. And as soon as he stopped, Garvey dropped on the floor with such a heavy, bomb-like weight that the tremble and thundering sound of the fall were felt and heard throughout the restaurant. Evelyn fell on top of Garvey, and her head landed on his chest, both nearly blacked out. The image was almost romantic were it not contrasted with Evelyn's bare ass and Garvey's half-erect penis next to her thigh.

A couple of other waiters and a person who looked to be the manager barged in, and just stood there dumbstruck at the scene.

"What the hell happened?!" the shocked manager yelled.

"This piece of shit was trying to rape that woman!" the waiter exclaimed, still obviously shaken by what happened.

"I wasn't..." said a frail-but-husky voice coming from the floor.

"Yes, you were, asshole!" retorted a nervous and angry Dylan.

"Alright, alright," said the manager. "Let's wait for them to regain full consciousness. Dylan, you call 911, and then you go back to work. I got this... Wait, leave me the taser."

Dylan gave his boss the taser and left the restroom.

"Alright, everybody, go back to work!" the manager ordered. "No, sorry," he said to a couple of women about to enter the restroom. "Sorry, ladies, but you're gonna have to hold it until we're done with this. Sorry, you'll get 25 percent off for the inconvenience. Rick, get their names and make sure to only charge 75 percent."

Rick nodded then went back to the restaurant along with the two women.

Things got calmer in the restroom, and Garvey and Evelyn were slowly coming out of their daze.

"Man, what have you done?" Brad, the manager, said in a low and patronizing voice as he was leaning against one of the sinks with the taser in his hand.

Garvey was slowly trying to get up, and Evelyn started moving...

"Don't!" said Brad in a cautionary tone with the taser still in his hand.

"I'm just trying to dust myself off, dude," reassured Garvey in a weakened voice. "Don't worry, I won't attempt anything."

"You better not!" Brad retorted. "You'd just be adding more years of you in the joint. The police are on their way."

Garvey slowly sat himself up, and leant against one of the stalls. An even more weakened Evelyn tried to do the same, then ended up laying her head on Garvey's shoulder.

"You're going right back to his arms?" a bewildered Brad asked with a chuckle.

"I didn't do anything to her…" said Garvey in a still-feeble voice.

"Right," Brad incredulously rejoined.

Garvey looked to Evelyn and said, "Tell him I didn't rape you."

"Or else what?" interjected Brad snidely. "Or you'll rape her again?" he continued with a grin.

A sudden heavy movement of men was heard escalating and approaching the restaurant, causing Garvey to feel some angst build up in his guts upon hearing it. After a few seconds, three men in uniform entered the restroom. The manager pointed to Garvey. And two of the men held him up and handcuffed him, while the third policeman told him he was under arrest and read him his Miranda rights.

Garvey was escorted out of the restaurant into a police car, and so was Evelyn by two of the remaining officers into another car. As the two were separated, Garvey shouted to Evelyn, "Tell the truth!" before he was put into the car. Evelyn remained placid, and was overwhelmed by what had happened just in the last five minutes.

Indeed, five minutes earlier, she was just sitting and having a nice meal with Garvey and thinking about her upcoming film. And then, there she was, in a police car, victim of a crime she was not even sure happened. It felt too surreal to her, and she spent the commute ridden with anxiety and foggy thinking.

As she arrived to the police station, she was asked to have a seat at the desk of an officer where she was told to make a deposition.

"So I understand this man forced himself on you?" the mustached officer asked.

"Yes, um, I think so," replied an inattentive Evelyn.

"What do you mean, you think so?"

"Uh, I don't know… I was in the bathroom, and… Yes, I guess he forced himself on me," said Evelyn, still looking confused.

"Right," said the officer while taking notes. "So, basically, he just came in, grabbed you, and tried to have intercourse with you?" he asked in a nasal voice and a dry, formal tone.

Evelyn remained silent for a few seconds, then said, "Yes."

"Did you, at any point, struggle or say, 'No'?"

"Sort of," she said, hesitantly.

"Meaning?"

Evelyn flustered as she tried to give a straight answer, which the policeman was impatiently awaiting, then said, while gesturing with her hands, "Look... We came together, we were having a nice meal. Then he told me-- then he told me to go to the bathroom. And then..."

"Hold on," the officer interjected. "Why did he tell you to go to the bathroom?"

"Yes! Exactly... I think, I think he was trying to initiate some role play or something," Evelyn explained unassertively.

"By forcing himself on you?" the officer asked with a raised eyebrow.

"He was trying to surprise me, I guess."

"By forcing himself on you?" the officer reiterated.

"I wouldn't call it that..." said Evelyn with a perplexed countenance.

Meanwhile, Garvey was undergoing the grilling of another officer in another room of that station.

"I was just initiating sex!" yelled Garvey in an exasperated manner which suggested he had been trying to explain himself for a while. "That's it! Did I explicitly ask for consent? No. But I kept telling her I was trying to surprise her, and as soon as she started going along, that little waiter prick tased me in the back! You should arrest *him* for assault, is what you should do!"

"Alright, calm down!" said the officer interrogating him, before leaving the room.

Garvey was sitting handcuffed in a room and watching his interrogator discussing with another policeman outside of the room. He couldn't hear them well.

The two cops then left and left Garvey alone with his thoughts in that room. He was staring distractedly onto the empty chair next to him, with the expression of a man thinking to himself, "How did I get here?"

And that is what Garvey was thinking, indeed. How did *he* get there? It all happened so fast. And it seemed that no matter how well Garvey tried to go about doing things, he would still mess it up. His social clumsiness vis-à-vis the opposite sex seemed incurable. But he still resolved to do something about it as soon as that latest episode was over.

About fifteen minutes later, the two officers were back. And the one who interrogated him said tersely, "You're free to go," as the other cop went to uncuff Garvey.

"What happened?" Garvey asked.

"No charges will be pressed against you, is what's happening," the interrogating officer replied. "Yours and Ms. West's accounts are pretty much identical. Seems to have been just a ham-handed way of surprising your girl. Next time, I suggest handcuffs in the privacy of your own home."

"I think I've had my fill of handcuffs for now," Garvey returned as he stood up.

"I meant for the lady," the officer noted as his colleague grinned.

"Right…" Garvey said. "Listen, I'd like to have a word with your captain. Is he here?"

"Why?" the officer asked warily.

"I just want to thank him for the service of this department, and apologize for the inconvenience," Garvey answered.

"No need for that," countered the officer while laying his hand forward as if to escort Garvey out.

"Listen, I'm a producer here in Hollywood with a nice home, and I pay a lot of your taxes. I just want to have a quick word with the man. Please," Garvey pleaded in a hushed but gravelly voice.

One of the policemen nodded to the other, who went to see the captain. Two minutes later, he came back, and told Garvey, "Please follow me."

The officer took Garvey to Captain Charlie Deck's office. Garvey went in, thanked the man and his department, before asking him to make sure what happened that day wouldn't leave the precinct in return for a yearly payment on Garvey's part.

Garvey left the PD five minutes later, and headed straight to Evelyn's.

He knocked on her door once, twice, thrice.

"Come on! I know you're here!" he shouted behind the door before laying a stronger fourth string of bangs. "I heard the guy say, 'We're taking her home.' Open!"

One of the neighbors passed by and looked at Garvey with suspicion and annoyance.

"She must be asleep. That's why I…" Garvey said to the neighbor, before banging on the door once more. "Come on!"

When Evelyn heard Garvey talk to the neighbor, she hurried and opened the door. Garvey got in while Evelyn smiled awkwardly to the still-suspicious neighbor.

Evelyn closed the door, and when she turned around, she saw Garvey sitting back nonchalantly on the couch, facing her:

"What up?" he said, casually.

"Um, 'what up?'" Evelyn asked rhetorically with somewhat of a sassy tone. "You *raped* me, that's what's up!" she continued with the same "excuse me" tone.

"And you almost threw me in the joint and had me lose my career because you wouldn't cooperate in that stall," Garvey responded.

"You fucking tried to rape me!" Evelyn reiterated louder and condescendingly.

"Hey, don't fucking talk to me that way!" said an angrier Garvey with a louder voice as he stood up from that couch and menacingly pointed his finger at Evelyn. "I didn't rape you and you know it!"

"You did! You tried to, asshole!" Evelyn gushed once more while throwing her arm toward Garvey.

Angry at what he saw as a bratty reaction, Garvey grabbed her forearm and strongly clenched it.

"Ow!" Evelyn sounded. "You're hurting me, asshole!"

Garvey slapped Evelyn, then tightened his grasp even more, and dragged her to the bathroom. "What are you doing?! Stop!" she yelled.

But Garvey struck her head with the palm of his hand and scornfully landed a backhanded slap on her face right after, and said, "Shut the fuck up."

Evelyn then just stopped moving, while her face betrayed the beginning of a cry. Garvey lowered himself near her level, saw a cowered-down Evelyn, then smirked, and said, "That's good..." before landing another powerful slap across her face for good measure.

"I'm going to teach you something tonight," he said with the same patronizing tone while firmly holding her forearm with one hand and lifting up the toilet seat with the other. "I'm going to teach you what actual rape is. You want to know what it is?"

He lowered himself again, and sarcastically leant his ear towards Evelyn, "What's that? You don't wanna?!"

Evelyn hadn't said anything. She just kept her head down with tears up her eyes while noticing the bulge swelling inside Garvey's pants. But Garvey pretended he heard her say something, then slapped her twice more and just as hard before pulling her hair and dragging her head down the toilet.

As he kept Evelyn's head down with one hand, he roughly pulled down her pants, then panties.

"Oh, yeah... Look at this..." he groaned hornily as he fondled her pussy. "You're even wet. What a whore. You're a fucking whore, aren't you?!" he grumbled angrily as he punched her in the back twice and gave her another slap on the head in contempt. "This is where you belong, bitch! You hear me?"

Evelyn remained silent while bent over with her head inside the toilet.

Garvey unzipped his swelling pants, pulled out his cock and began rubbing it against Evelyn's moist pussy, before he spat on her asshole and tried to shove his member in forcefully.

"Ooow!" Evelyn screamed in pain as she jumped and twitched.

"Stay still, bitch!" ordered Garvey as he struck her upper back with the side of his fist. "You're not worthy of being fucked from the front. Your other hole will do just as well," he said with the heavy, noisy breathing of a horny, overweight man. "Come on, get in!" he continued as he tried to ram his penis in, until he did.

Garvey availed himself of Evelyn's behind for three uninterrupted minutes until he came inside her while letting out a powerful roar. He pulled her hair even harder during his orgasm.

Evelyn couldn't be heard emitting so much as a moan throughout the three minutes.

When the man was done, he pulled, wiped his member Evelyn's her butt, got up, and casually dropped the toilet seat on her head and tauntingly flushed the toilet as he let out a chuckle, before leaving the bathroom, and the house.

Garvey got to his car, sighed in relief, and said, "Oh, yeah, that felt good," then drove away.

Once Garvey got home, he sat down and began thinking about what he had done. He sighed and closed his eyes in a "here we go again" fashion once he realized he needed to lawyer up and go through the damage-control dance once again. He looked distantly into the void and thought to himself, "Why am I doing this?" before letting a little laugh at himself.

Ten seconds later, he snapped out of his contemplation, and said in his head, "Okay, first things first. I need to get Stuart oiled up and ready—nay, eager—to get down to business."

Garvey picked up the phone, and was about to call his assistant, but then looked at the time, and decided to text her the following instead: "I want you and Helda in my office first thing tomorrow (8:45)"

He then dropped the phone on a table casually, grabbed a bottle of scotch, and flung himself on the couch. He drank and looked at the ceiling pensively while thinking about how he had just lived through the craziest day of his life.

At that same moment, Evelyn was, likewise, laying on her couch placidly looking at her TV but not watching what was in it; her mind was miles away.

The rapist and his victim dozed off at the same moment.

* * * *

The next day, at 8:47 a.m., someone knocked on the door to Garvey's office.

"One second!" Garvey exclaimed while he was frantically typing on his computer. He was trying to finish his thought. The last paragraph he typed read, "And that, ladies, is how I knew she craved it all along. She never said so, and I never expected her to do. But you and I know that she did. And so I did what I had to do, out of love… rough love," under a post titled, "Coming Clean: What VelvetEglantine Truly Did (TRUE STORY)" whose content was wildly similar to what had happened the night before.

Garvey clicked on 'Save,' and planned on posting it later.

"Come in!" he said as he closed his laptop.

Helda and Sanjeep opened the door and came in.

"There they are, my two favorite sunrays!" Garvey enthused with a smile and a welcoming-but-pompous tone.

The two women responded with an embarrassed and somewhat uncomfortable smile, and sat down.

"How are you, Mr. Feinstein?" Helda politely asked.

"Great, great," Garvey replied rather unconvincingly. "Well, not so great, actually, which is why you're here."

*"Another 'incident'?" asked Helda with a knowing half-smile, raised eyebrow and the overall expression of a skeptical mother interrogating her mischievous son.

"Well… Yeah, that's exactly what it is," he answered while putting his five fingertips against his other five fingertips, making a pyramid with his hands, and striking a thoughtful and solemn pose. "But this one is a little more serious—or has the potential to be—which is why I'm directly sending my attorney to play catcher and control damage rather than you. However, this'll be his first mission, and a very sensitive one. Which is why I need someone to grease his gears beforehand, to make him more excited and more willing to get in there, you know? And that 'someone' will be the two of you."

There was a three-second bout of silence, during which a puzzled and concerned Sanjeep turned to Helda, who then asked:

"Um, grease his gears?"

"Yeah! Make him... more eager to do it, you know? In ways that only a woman could, you follow me?" he replied intently.

"I'm afraid I am," Helda muttered apprehensively as she adjusted herself in her seat.

Garvey heard that and went on to reassure the women.

"Listen, you don't have to... touch him, or any of that," he said. "But you could, I don't know, pop a couple more buttons off that blouse." Garvey pointed to Sanjeep's blouse as he said that, before he turned to Helda, pointed to her skirt, and said, "Is that skirt arriving to your knees? What are you, a schoolmarm? Stuart needs to see some skin, so he can have a love for life to, you know, go ahead and do his thing, do his job!" Garvey passionately explained.

The producer went on to sing the praises of women arousing men, claiming that they pushed said men to "take care of business," in a zealously preachy manner replete with hand gesturing. The two women sat and watched the whole spiel while slightly overwhelmed and not knowing what to think.

When Garvey was done with his sermon, there was a short-but-heavy moment of silence, which Helda was about to break—Sanjeep was too shy to say anything—by opening her mouth and talk. But Garvey interrupted her beforehand:

"And that's an order. I don't want any discussion about it. I'm giving this instruction as your boss, as something you're going to do as part of your job," he ruled in a firmer tone. "Today, you're going to Mr. Aaronsohn's office... Hold on, let me check if he's there first."

Garvey picked the phoned and called Stuart. He asked whether his assistants could come pay him a visit regarding an incident he needed him to deal with. "Yes, of the nature we talked about the other day," Garvey replied during the conversation, before asking him where he was.

When Garvey hung up, he told his assistants, "Yes, you're going to his office. Helda knows where it is. You're going there, and you're gonna show him some tits and ass! You're gonna... Okay, stand up," he said before he stood up himself, went near Helda, and sat on the desk in front of her.

Helda stood up with apparent reluctance.

"Alright, so what do we got here..." said Garvey as he probingly eyed his assistant up and down.

"Is this really necessary?" Helda asked.

"Yes!" Garvey replied swiftly and curtly as he looked her seriously in the eye. "It is. So... Yeah, so you're wearing something like, uh, something like that blouse on Sanjeep and you unbutton it. Either that or something else that shows cleavage. You see the general image?"

Helda nodded with the same reluctance, while Sanjeep was peaking glances at the whole scene shyly from her seat.

"Hmm, yeah..." Garvey continued. "So you're going to show some of that bosom. And the hair, you're gonna have to let it all down, like flowing. And the– turn around. Yeah, show more of that ass. Oh, yeah, wear something tighter. You see the general idea?"

At that moment, Sanjeep's mouth was agape in astonishment as she put her hand over her eyebrow and displayed an uncomfortable body language. The agape mouth was partly due to Garvey's increasingly conspicuous erection being pitched from under his pants while he was handling Helda.

"... And, of course, you keep the heels on. Okay, your turn, 'Jeep! Come on up."

Sanjeep stood up, and Garvey went up to her in slow, but firm steps. He approached his heavy, whale-like body, then his heavy-breathing face to her throat until his stubble touched her face. Garvey took a couple of sniffs, then said, "I like this perfume. You put more of it when you go see Stuart."

Sanjeep had her eyes closed the whole time Garvey had his face near her neck. And when he told her to put more of that perfume, she nodded.

Garvey then grabbed her butt and turned her around, and said, "Yeah, you keep that... You put on something similar, just shorter. Alright?"

Sanjeep nervously nodded again, while Helda sat there watching the whole scene with less discomfort than Sanjeep but with a facial expression that was constantly verging on an eye-roll.

But inside, both women were uneasy and overwhelmed at the same time, albeit to different degrees. Despite his creepiness, Garvey often managed to have an overwhelming presence that could prompt the people around him to just go along with him and with whatever he wanted to do. Part of that was simply the positional authority he most often had over these people, the authority that came with him being the boss, the person that outranked them in the hierarchy, and all the concomitant aura of power. But Garvey seemed to have a little more than that—his personality, as awkward and socially clueless as it often was, still managed to act as a pole of gravity on those who surrounded him, even when those people repulsed by him.

Garvey pursued his pep talk on what the two women should do and how to behave around Stuart:

"And so," he clarified, "if you ever accidentally touch him, or rub yourself on him, that's fine, it happens. And if he does it himself, that's what men do. Just remember, you're there to please him! That's the main mission of that visit. Well, that, and... and the incident Stuart's going to deal with." Garvey paused for a few seconds, the continued. "A woman by the name of Evelyn West. You know her, right?"

Both women nodded.

"Right. I'll leave you her info that you'll give to Mr. Aaronsohn. Yeah, that woman that Sanjeep pitched a while ago needs to be caught now, by him. She needs to be caught because we had an encounter that might be construed as 'a little forceful' by her," said Garvey while using airquotes with his hand. "And so, Stuart will hopefully convince her that it's in her best interest not to go any further with this and... Well, Stu will know what to do. You just go to him, cozy up to him, tell him what I told you about the incident, and he'll take it from there."

The women replied with a cautious, "Okay," then Garvey continued:

"So that's pretty much it," he concluded. "Give him a briefing on the story while being foxy and not saying, 'No'."

"Not saying, 'No'?" Helda warily asked, hoping for more details.

"Yeah!" her boss asserted. "With all that entails! I want the guy pleased! I want him pleased enough to go to that broad's house with a bounce in his step. If he likes what he sees in you, and wants to do something, let him! You're my assistants; assist me! Also, you're women, so do your thing. And sometimes, you don't just do; you're done to."

Sanjeep felt a little tingle in her spine as she heard and processed Garvey's last sentence. Of all her emotionally conflicting moments towards her boss, this was among the most intense she had. The more dignified part of her hated the man for the way he dehumanized and objectified both her and Helda, and the way he aggressively pushed them to make use of their sex appeal, making them feel like mere things whose primary usefulness was the pleasure of men, of men more powerful than they were. And that dignified, self-respecting part of her hated it.

Yet, the baser parts of her brain seemed to relish those very things, and made her more compliant and agreeable in the face of the man's transgressions. She would have probably complied anyway because she didn't want to lose her job, but more begrudgingly so.

And Helda felt more-or-less the same way.

"Alright, time to go," Garvey instructed with zest as he slapped his hands together and rubbed them.

As the two women turned around, Garvey spanked their butts and told them to "work it" with attempted playfulness. Sanjeep felt another chill throughout her body as he did that.

Once the women left, Garvey called the lawyer and made sure he was going to see and deal with Evelyn that day. Stuart reassured him that he would and that Garvey had nothing to worry about. "I won't let her get unreasonable," he said. "It's in her best interest not to be."

Garvey approvingly nodded behind the phone and thanked him, then alluded to Stuart that he could have his way with his two assistants. "They're very friendly," Garvey affirmed. "They'll be very friendly. And they won't rebuff you, you follow me? They're yours."

"I think I am," Stuart replied with a smile. "Though I don't think that will be necessary."

"It's up to you, buddy."

Garvey hung up, then felt a shudder of excitement at what that day could potentially bring. He then went to get himself ready for the meeting he had with his brother and five other co-producers on Almóndolar's movie at ten.

As Garvey's meeting began, the women were on their way to Stuart's office. Both were grasped with apprehension all along the way.

Stuart opened the door with a smile, welcomed the assistants in, who smiled back and came strutting into the room with their short skirts, tight, low-cut upper garments, and high heels. Sanjeep's gait was a little more awkward than Helda's, but she still managed to seduce Stuart who snuck a furtive leer at the women's behinds and legs as they were headed to take a seat.

Helda began by thanking Stuart for receiving them, before giving him a rundown on the situation, as per Garvey's instructions. Stuart was listening and taking notes while occasionally glancing at Helda and Sanjeep's cleavage.

Stuart then stood up, went up near Helda and said, "So, if I understand correctly, this actress is going to be on Mr. Feinstein upcoming film." Stuart was standing so close to Helda that his penis rubbed against her shoulder a few times when he said that.

Helda felt Stuart's member against her, but didn't react to it, and answered the man as if nothing were happening. "Yes, that is correct," she said.

"Right, right," Stuart said as he was scratching his chin.

At that moment, the thirty-something lawyer was reminded of Garvey's words that the women wouldn't say, "No," and that they were his. So he just had a "what the heck" moment in his head, and straightforwardly unzipped his pants, pulled out his swollen penis, and downright told Helda to "suck [his] dick."

Helda recoiled a little and said, "What?"

Stuart didn't say anything. Instead, he just slowly pushed Helda's head down with one hand, and inserted his member inside her mouth with the other, then kept on directing her head for two minutes until he groaned and filled her with hot semen. He then kept his hand over her mouth and jaw and looked at her intently as if to say, "You know what you are supposed to do," until she did. He gave her two slight, approving taps on her lower cheek, zipped his pants back up, took his car keys, a folder, and as he was leaving, said, "You just shut the door on your way out, ladies. And don't bother snooping in my stuff before you do; there's a camera."

Twenty minutes later, Stuart arrived to Evelyn's. He parked his car in front of her house, heaved a sigh of apprehension, got out of the car, and headed to her door. He knocked once, twice, then a woman's voice from the inside asked:

"Who's there?"

"Stuart Aaronsohn, attorney of law," the man replied. "I'd like to have a word with you."

There was no response from Evelyn for ten full seconds. Then, she opened the door.

"How can I help you?" she asked, coldly.

"I'm here on behalf of Garvey Fei…"

Stuart hadn't finished his sentence that Evelyn pushed the door shut almost reflexively, but Stuart siwftly pushed back just before the door closed.

"I just want to talk to you," he reassured her as he was holding the door open.

"I don't!" Evelyn responded with the same cold, hostile tone.

"This kind of attitude is not going to help anybody," the lawyer said calmly. "Hear me out…"

"No," she interjected with a quieter voice but the same hostile tone.

"Hear me out!" Stuart reiterated loudly, before he pleaded: "Listen… I just have something to say. I'll say it in three minutes, then I'll leave. All I ask is you sit down and listen to what I have to say. Please."

Evelyn stayed silent for a few seconds, then went to sit down on her couch and told Stuart to close the door behind him.

Stuart closed the door then followed Evelyn to the living room and sat down on the armchair in front of her.

"I understand there's been an incident with Mr. Garvey Feinstein yesterday," Stuart prefaced his talk.

"Look, I know where this is going," a jaded-sounding Evelyn interrupted. "I know what you're going to propose."

"What am I going to propose?" Stuart asked.

"You're going to tell me it's in my interest to take the hush money and shut up about what happened. I've been through this. I don't want your money," an unusually assertive and solemn Evelyn said.

Stuart paused, then asked, "How are you gonna prove the-- whatever happened, then?"

"I don't want to prosecute him either," she replied.

"So, if you don't want money, and you don't want to have him punished by the law, then what do you want?" the lawyer asked, perplexed.

"I want Garvey," she answered. "I want him to come and talk to me, to come and explain himself."

"Why didn't you just call him then?" Stuart asked.

"I wanted him to want to do that."

Silence ensued, then Stuart said, "Well, I guess my work here is done," as he slapped his hand on his knee. He thanked Evelyn for her cooperation, then left.

Once back to his practice, Stuart called Garvey, and informed him that Evelyn wanted to see him. Garvey was a little surprised, and imparted to Stuart that that felt like a trap Evelyn was trying to set for him.

"I don't know..." responded Stuart. "The woman sounded genuine to me. Listen, you don't have to go. And if you ever do, my advice would be to never explicitly admit what you did to her yesterday in your conversations."

"You think she's going to wiretap me or something?" a worried Garvey asked.

"Again, I don't know. But just to be on the safe side, do as I said."

"Alright, thanks," the producer said before he hung up.

Garvey was worried, and rightly so. He had left a good deal of skeletons on his way thus far, and one of them was bound to come and haunt him sooner or later. The problem was that he didn't know which one, or when.

But still, he knew he had to keep going and that worrying about his past every step of the way was counterproductive. In the immediate, he had to deal with Evelyn. And so, there he went.

First, he texted her to ask if she was home, and she answered with a terse, "Yes."

A half an hour later, he was in front of Evelyn's door. He knocked, she opened, he entered and stood in her living room with a cautious look on his face. He then began to go over her furniture while trying to display a casual attitude, as if he were interested in the knick-knacks and the vases on them.

"What are you doing?" Evelyn asked.

Garvey turned around, went up to her, made a sniffing gesture with his nose, and said, "I'm allergic to bugs. Put your hands up…"

Evelyn rolled her eyes, and said, "Jesus" in disbelief and ridicule, but raised her hands nevertheless. Garvey roughly patted and groped her body looking for bugs, from top to bottom, while spending extra seconds on the chest and thigh areas.

"You're good," Garvey proclaimed.

"Thank you," Evelyn replied sarcastically.

Garvey stepped back after his inspection, then confided with an almost apologetic tone, "I had to do it. You never know, you know?"

"I know," Evelyn replied with the beginning of a smile, feeling almost endeared by Garvey's eccentric ways.

The whole vibe between Garvey and Evelyn was that of a couple five years into a marriage, very comfortable with each other, and not one of a rapist and a victim who still didn't know each other all that well. The casualness of their interaction may have appeared almost obscene to an onlooker, given what had happened a day ago. But knowing Garvey's "natural" proclivities of forcing himself on women, and knowing how Evelyn actually experienced the event, one could begin to explain it.

Garvey headed to the couch with a devil-may-care attitude and sat himself on it with a manspread and arm-spread on its backrest that would have irritated even the least feminist of women.

"So what did you want to see me for?" he asked, with the same nonchalant attitude.

"I didn't," she said. "Who told you that?"

"Stuart."

"Well, he was wrong."

Garvey understood that Evelyn didn't want to sound like she wanted him, so he went along with that.

"Okay," he conciliatorily said. "How about you tell me how you've been feeling instead?"

Garvey tapped on the couch next to him, as if to call Evelyn to sit there and talk it out. Evelyn sat next to him, took a deep breath, then, with a serious air, said as she looked at the ground, "What you did to me the other day..."

"I'm sorry," Garvey solemnly declared. "I'm truly sorry."

"Okay. But let me finish this first..." Evelyn replied as she was still trying to recollect her thoughts. "The amount of violence I received was one I've never been subject to in my entire life. And I hated it. I hated the violence." Evelyn paused for a while as if to ponder on whether it was a good idea to share what was about to follow or not, but went on nonetheless. "But with that violence came an incredible amount of passion," she intimated slowly and uncomfortably, "passion that was directed at me, solely for me, that I was the cause of. And this was also a first for me. I'm ashamed of myself for saying that, but I loved that passion, and I loved being the center of it and the recipient of it. And I think if someone goes as far as doing all that to you, then they must feel something towards you, or care about you... Right?"

Garvey looked at the floor pensively for a moment, then raised his head and looked at Evelyn and said, "So you're not going to press charges?"

Evelyn grabbed a small pillow on the couch and threw it at Garvey in anger, who then exclaimed, "Okay! Okay! Listen, of course I felt-- You're asking me if I did what I did because I had some underlying feelings towards you, besides lust... Is that it?"

"Yes."

"Well, I'm not gonna lie," Garvey confided. "At that moment, when you were completely in my grasp, I felt like you were truly, completely mine. And yeah, I liked that feeling of making you mine."

Evelyn let out an endeared smile as if Garvey had just told her he enjoyed buying flowers and chocolate. And Garvey smiled back at her.

"And...?"

"And I didn't want that to finish. Still don't," he said. "I may have expressed my desire for you a little too aggressively and hurtfully. And I'm sorry for that. But the desire is still there, and I don't want it to end."

Evelyn kept silent, hanging at Garvey's words.

"Alright, I gotta go!" Garvey concluded as he slapped his hands and got up.

Evelyn stood along with him. Garvey kissed her near her mouth, said he would call her, casually but vigorously slapped her butt, then headed for the door.

As he opened the door, Evelyn asked when they would the shooting of her upcoming film start, and Garvey answered it was going to be the following week.

On his way to the car, Garvey wondered if Evelyn was only playing nice so as to not rock the boat and keep her part for the movie. He suspected she was, which he found unfortunate, given that he genuinely liked her and liked the idea of making her his.

Regardless of whether it was going to work out with the aspiring actress or not, Garvey knew he had too many problems with the opposite sex, too many skeletons, so many that it could not have been a coincidence—it wasn't "them"; it was him. Pitchers, catchers, lawyers… Any man who needed this many crutches to keep his social interactions from ruining his life had to have something wrong with him. And while Garvey never openly admitted this much to himself, he still knew he had to do something to improve his social skills before it all blew up in his face.

※ ※ ※ ※

When Garvey got home, he went online and Googled "social skills women." An array of articles full of dating advice turned up—some with plain, generic tips along the lines of "make her laugh" and "be alpha," among other nerdier and more headache-inducing ones such as, "look for IOIs then lay an indirect opener and throw a push/pull on her before demanding compliance while keeping some attainability as to not send her into auto-rejection."

Garvey read a couple of articles, then said, "I'm too rich for this shit." He then went on to type, "hire pick up artist." A slew of pick-up artists offering their "hands-on" services appeared. Garvey picked one up from Los Angeles, and called him.

"Hi, is this Mastery?"

"This is him," Mastery said. "How can I help you?"

"I, uh, I need some help in approaching the females and making them have sex with me without it turning into a potential criminal case. Can you do that?" Garvey asked.

"Totally," swiftly and enthusiastically answered Mastery.

"Great. So how do we start? You come over and we talk first, or do we go directly 'in-field'?" Garvey asked.

"Well, first, I'm gonna need to see where you're at, your fundamentals, your traits," the guru explained. "And then we'll take it from there. So, yeah, I'm gonna need to talk to you a little first, and then we'll move on to the in-field."

"Okay, you're the expert!" Garvey deferred. "So can you come over tomorrow to my studio? I'm in LA, too."

The two men agreed on the meeting, with Garvey requesting from the PUA—Justin—not to introduce himself as such when he would come to the studios.

As Garvey hung up, he sighed deeply in anticipation of potentially eventful and hectic days ahead. He then ate, washed, and went to bed directly.

The day after, Garvey spent the morning with Moody Alan, as the two men checked on a soon-to-be shooting set out in the desert for their upcoming film.

At 1 p.m., Garvey was back in his office, and Sanjeep rang his phone and informed him that a young man named Justin wanted to see him. Garvey told her to let him in.

A smooth and mysterious-looking man in his late twenties came in wearing a hat that had a feather on, longish brown hair flowing out of it, sunglasses, a soul patch, an unbuttoned shirt, a necklace, worn-out jeans, and wingtip boots.

"What's up, Mr. Feinstein?" he greeted with a warm tone and a velvet voice as he took off his glasses and laid out his hand.

Garvey stood from his chair just enough to reach the man's hand and shake it with a smile, and told him to have a seat.

"Is that… part of your 'game'?" Garvey asked as he pointed to Justin's appearance.

"It's called 'peacocking'," the young man answered confidently. "It gives you character. It makes you look like a somebody."

A seemingly impressed Garvey nodded repeatedly and frowned his mouth in approval, then asked, "And that's what the ladies want, a somebody with character?"

"Yup," Justin swiftly replied. "Though they'd still be open for a fling or more with a nobody with character or a somebody without. But you have to be at least one."

Garvey shook his head in inspiration again. "So how do I know if I have either, or both?" he inquired.

"You're at least one, that's for sure," Justin replied.

"Which one?"

"The 'somebody'?" the PUA answered with a tone and countenance that read, "Duh." "You're a Hollywood producer. That alone makes you bangable—excuse the French."

Garvey felt a rush of pride at that moment and was almost embarrassed. He then asked with a contained smile, "What about the 'character' part?"

"Well," Justin said, "from what I gather from your talk on potential criminal cases, you don't really lack character. If anything, you have too much of it, or don't channel it correctly. So the main challenge here would be to turn that mutual attraction between you and the woman in question into something concrete in a smooth, socially gracious way. In other words, make the transition from 'no relationship' to 'relationship,' from meeting to mating, as non-messy as possible."

"And is that what you guys call 'game,' how to take things from 'meeting to mating'?" Garvey asked while using airquotes.

"Yup, that's pretty much what game is," Justin confided. "There's your game, and there's your fundamentals."

"'Fundamentals'?"

"The Fundamentals are your status—how much of a somebody you are, how much influence, social power, wealth, character, etc.—plus looks. Basically, how strong, original, interesting, or fun you come off. They're sort of like your passive traits," Justin explained. "Now, you have enough of the first two that looks won't matter all that much in your case, though your height and overall size are certainly a plus."

"Hmm, interesting," Garvey commented. "So when do we start, and how much do you charge?"

Justin informed Garvey of his free days that week as well as his fees—$70 per in-field hour, 50 for out of field—and the two men agreed to start the day after. Justin advised Garvey to wear a nice, dark shirt, as well as his "shiniest watch and shoes."

The following day, Justin suggested he sees Garvey for a "pep meeting" to "pump [him] up" behind closed doors before getting in the arena. Garvey told him to just come by his studio.

Once with Garvey again, the young instructor noted, "The Pep Meeting will put you in the right mood and the right disposition to get your groove on and go pick up some chicks. It primes you psychologically for pick-up. So here's what we're gonna do... Do you have a mirror?"

Garvey pointed to the mirror.

Garvey and Justin then stood in front of it, and, as per the instructions of Justin, began to enthusiastically and rhetorically exclaim, "Who's got swag?!" and "I got swag!"

"Do you got swag?!" Justin yelled with passion.

"Hell, yeah, I do!" Garvey yelled back as he adopted a prideful stance in what became a frenzied exchange. "I got tons of swag!"

"You're the boss of Hollywood, dog!" Justin affirmed. "Are you feeling your balls recharging right now?"

"Yeah!" Garvey affirmed back with antagonistic, juvenile zeal, before grabbing his scrotum in a machistic display of defiance and dominance.

Then, as Garvey raised his head while still having his typical dumb-looking, smug smile, he noticed Justin's worried and awkward gaze facing the door. Garvey turned around, and saw his assistant Helda standing there along with Pedro Almóndolar. The Hollywood producer let go of his crotch, and tried as best he could to hide his uttermost embarrassment, before scolding his assistant.

"Whatever happened to the intercom?!" he bawled. "Or to knocking?!"

"I'm sorry," a somewhat flustered and apologetic Helda replied. "I knocked, but you didn't answer. And when I heard…"

"Alright, alright…" Garvey interrupted before turning to Pedro and laying his hand to shake his while switching tones. "Pedro, how are you doing?"

"Doing great, Garvey. How are you?" Pedro replied then returned the question in a professional tone.

"Fine, fine. Look, I'm sorry I'm really busy this morning. You should've called, man. If you're available this afternoon, after lunch, I'll be more than happy to have you," Garvey proposed with a friendly demeanor and a tap on Pedro's shoulder.

"That's okay. I only came by because I was around anyway," Pedro replied in his still-heavy Spanish accent. "Yes, after lunch works for me."

Garvey thanked Pedro and his assistant before the two left his office. And two minutes later, he hit the road with Justin.

Justin told him they would be doing Day Game that day.

"What's that?" Garvey asked.

"It's just approaching women during the day," Justin explained. "Now, it has its pros and cons. For a guy who's new to approaching, daytime can be a little more intimidating. You can't just disappear into the haze of darkness, anonymity, and alcohol the night offers. Nor do you have the social context of nighttime venues, where people are there in the first place to socialize and meet new people."

"Why d'you get me out in the day for then?!" Garvey exclaimed with a hint of brattiness in his voice.

"Because women are less on their guard during the day, less hostile," Justin calmly answered, "especially those who aren't in an obvious hurry to go somewhere. They get approached less, partly because fewer guys have the socializing momentum or the liquid courage in their veins to do the approaching. At night, they're *expecting* to be hit on, so they're more guarded, even at the beginning of the night, so they'll be a little more defensive and a little more selective, especially after every sloppy, tipsy guy and his brother made a pass at them."

"So what if they're more selective?" Garvey asked. "I'm a top-notch guy anyway!"

"You may be in the studio," an unfazed Justin explained. "But in some club, or out in the street to at least half the people, you're just some dude. But even with that and everything I said before in mind, you'll find yourself able to hit it off with women you'd normally almost never be able to approach at night. The girl who goes out in a tiny sequined dress, dances with three of her girlfriends, and rejects every guy who comes within a twenty-foot radius of her is far more approachable dressed down during the day. Especially that many of them are only out there in the nightclub to show off and seek male validation and attention."

"Hmm, I see," a genuinely interested Garvey uttered. "So where are we headed?"

"Echo Park!"

"Woo-hoo!" Garvey celebrated half-sarcastically.

"I'm liking the energy!" a smiling Justin commented.

Fifteen minutes later, the two men were ambling through the park. Justin explained that the best targets were—in addition to being cute, pretty, beautiful, or sexy—those who didn't seem to be in a hurry, and those who were either alone or with just one female friend.

"Why *female* friend?" Garvey asked.

"Two reasons," Justin premised with the same self-assured, been-there-done-that tone: "The girlfriend is more likely to be interested in your wingman—yours truly—hitting on her or at least platonically handling her. Because that's basically what the wingman often does: he handles the other people. And chicks are just more open to being handled than dudes are. Second, a dude is much more likely to be her boyfriend than a female is. And finally, even guy *friends* just aren't that fond of seeing some other dude hitting on the chick they're with. Because, you know, these 'friends' are more often than not just friend-*zoned*, really, hoping to get out of it someday. Hope springs eternal in the human breast…"

"Speaking of human breast," Garvey interjected as he nudged Justin and pointed to a busty girl jogging by with earphones in her ears.

"Nice," Justin commented. "But see, that's the kind of 'hurried' you want to avoid. A hurried female has like a 90 percent rejection rate in the best of times and with the best of games. If she's running, then don't even bother."

"I see, I see…" said Garvey as he kept looking around him with his mouth slightly agape.

"Dude, what are you doing?" Justin called out. "Don't look around you like that like a thirsty jackal. You're going to creep the girls away before we even begin!"

"Well, I am thirsty," remarked Garvey.

"I know, but… fake it till you make it, bro," the PUA advised, before pointing his head to two young women seated on a bench. "Check those two."

Justin told Garvey to follow his lead, and suggested he would do the talking that first time. Garvey asked what was his pick-up line; Justin looked at Garvey, lowered his shades, and said, "Hi" with a grin. Garvey grinned back in approval and admiration.

The two men walked to the seated women. On their way, Garvey could be heard saying to himself, "I got swag."

Once there, Justin took off his sunglasses, said hi with a warm smile, and engaged the women.

"Hi! I know this is kind of random, but I just have to tell you you're both really cute. I couldn't help myself but stop," the young man said. "Aren't they, Garvey?"

The two men sat down and introduced themselves.

"Hi, I'm Justin, and this is my friend Garvey," Justin said as he laid out his hand.

"I'm a Hollywood producer," Garvey promptly blurted out.

The two girls' eyes lit up as they directed their attention to Garvey, and one of them said, "Wow. Really?" Garvey nodded, then the impressed girl continued, "What movies did you produce?"

Garvey laid his elbow on the backrest of the bench, and began nonchalantly talking about the movies he produced, the famous directors and actors he had worked with, and his personal touch on several renowned films.

"You know that scene from Pope Friction where they talk about bologna sandwich in the car?" he rhetorically asked with the same nonchalant and slightly smug tone. "My idea."

The woman looked impressed, while Justin shook his head. The second one turned to Justin and asked him if he worked for Garvey.

"More like *with* Garvey," Justin replied.

Justin engaged the other woman, who found him cute. And the two "couples" chatted for a few minutes, until the pick-up guru said they had to get going and suggested the girls leave their numbers, which they did.

Garvey left with a big smile on his face, but Justin was less pleased. Garvey looked at Justin, and asked:

"What's with the long face? You got your number, didn't you?"

"Dude," Justin replied, "you shouldn't have that crutch!"

"What crutch?" Garvey asked defensively.

"The Hollywood crutch!" Justin yelled. "You told the girl you not only produced a Tartino movie, but wrote the dialogues on one of the most epic scenes in history!"

"Yeah, I might have exaggerated a bit on this one," Garvey confessed.

"It doesn't matter," Justin retorted. "Relying on your fame, influence, and that kind of positional authority is a *huge* crutch. It's like playing on Super Easy Mode. And that's not how you learn."

"Listen, I'm not here to become a master seducer. I only want to talk to a girl and get her to bed without the threats and legal stuff. I just want to pick up chicks with more tact, you know, lead the thing from meeting to mating, as you said, without too much physical force or incidents." Garvey explained. "And I'm getting there. I observed your ways of opening them, getting them to smile, be receptive, that's all good. That's what I want to learn. Now, I just want to get them from there to on my cock."

Justin paused, slightly shook his head with a chuckle, then said while smiling, "Alright. We'll get you there," as Garvey nodded along. "But I still think your Hollywood status is way too big a crutch."

"Okay, then give me a smaller crutch!"

Justin paused for a second, then said, "Preselection."

"What's that?"

Justin began explaining, but Garvey had a hard time following. So after two minutes, the young man just summed it up as "being seen with a hot or pretty chick," claiming this would make women want Garvey more and be more receptive to him. It was still a fairly big crutch, Justin maintained, but not as big as relying on Hollywood status.

When Garvey finally grasped what that was about, he thought about it for a few seconds, then said with a determined attitude, "Say no more."

"What?" asked a wary Justin.

"I got just the right female!" declared Garvey with a sly and knowing expression followed by a smirk.

In the meantime, Helda was sitting on a couch in the studio sipping some coffee and taking a break from dealing with the actors and taking messages for Garvey. Her phone rang and she picked up:

"Hello, Mr. Feinstein," she answered. "Uh, tonight? (...) But I'll be working all afternoon. (...) What? (...) Um, I don't know. (...) Uhh..."

That was her whole conversation with Garvey before she hung up with a distressed look on her face. Garvey had just asked her to get herself ready for a night out with him in some venue in Los Angeles, because he needed "someone to parade." He told her she could take the afternoon off, let Sanjeep take care of things, and that he would call her at 8:30 p.m.

"... and so you should be ready by then," Garvey instructed. "Oh, yeah, and you're advised to dress like a slut."

Garvey hung up, then gave Justin an assured and positive, "Done."

"Cool," responded Justin with an approving nod and a smile.

Garvey nodded and smiled along, making two dudes nodding and smiling contentedly in the middle of Echo Park.

"So, you got any idea where we should head tonight?" Garvey asked.

"Yeah, there's this place called 'Area.' It's a great venue, like a classy nightclub. You got tables, cocktails and all, where you can sit with your girl, and you also got a bar and a dancefloor around which you can do some pick-up. Perfect place for preselection game," Justin described.

In response, Garvey nodded slowly with that same approving smile and half-closed eyes, before exclaiming with the happiness of a child who had just got his toys, "I got swag!" and Justin replying paternalistically with the same smile, "You sure do."

Garvey was thrilled and energized about that night. He had the feeling that things were truly looking up for him, and felt rare, genuine happiness at that moment. It was one of those moments in life he felt on top of the world: business was going great, he was in the process of getting better at dealing with the opposite sex, and he had a name and status in society most men only dreamt of. At that particular moment, his only wish was to have a longer penis, but that, he planned to deal with later on.

Fifteen minutes later, Garvey parted ways with Justin, whom he planned to meet again that evening at eight.

Sure enough, at eight o'clock, Justin was back in Hollywood. Garvey left his name to the guards to let him in. And Justin drove through the studios, and parked by Garvey's. It was his third time there, but was still amazed by the magnitude and significance of the place that still gave him that dizzying feeling of surrealism each time he went there.

The young man rang to Garvey, and Garvey told him to come up in. Justin knocked, and was invited in. As he entered, he saw Garvey laying on the couch of his large office watching a French film by the name of *Non-Reversible*.

"Hey, there!" Justin greeted.

"Hey," said Garvey as he sat himself up.

"You a fan of French flicks?" Justin asked casually as he was headed to one of the chairs.

"Not particularly," Garvey replied. "But this one has some very great scenes."

Justin nodded. Then Garvey continued:

"Alright, give me five to ten to get myself ready," he said as he stood up and headed for the adjacent room. "So this is like a semi-classy place, right?"

"Yup. Just a blazer and a nice shirt will do," Justin answered. "And throw in some peacocking if you have any."

"Gotcha!"

Ten minutes later, a nice-looking Feinstein came back in a navy-blue shirt, a chain necklace of medium thickness, nice dark pants and shoes, and his favorite ring, and enthused with a smirk, "Let's get on it!" while pointing both his fingers to Justin in a Fonzie-like fashion.

Justin just nodded approvingly while sporting a wide smile and saying, "Nice!" And even though that last move from Garvey looked cheesy to him, he was still rather endeared by the grown man's juvenile enthusiasm.

And Garvey was indeed at the height of his excitement. Some of that came from his apprehension that he might mess up again, but also from the prospect of finally making peace with women, and being able to interact with his romantic and sexual prospects without an entire team of baseball players around him to pick up the pieces, and without the looming risk of it turning into a criminal matter.

On their way out, Garvey told Justin they would be going in the PUA's car, and that Garvey would be covering gas and then some. He then texted Helda, "We're on our way. Call you when we're there."

And on their way they were.

"Damn! I'm so hyped!" Garvey exclaimed.

"I bet you are!" Justin responded with a smile. "Who's got swag?"

"I do!" Garvey cried.

"I didn't hear ya!"

"I got swag!" Garvey brashly blustered again. "Oh, yeah, we're dropping by Helda's first. We're picking her up. Just follow my directions."

"Okay."

Ten minutes later, the two men were parked in front of Helda's.

Garvey received a text back from her asking him to duck down in the car so he couldn't be seen. Garvey asked why, and Helda texted back, "Please do it! Just do it, I'll explain later. Pls!!"

Helda told her boyfriend Roy she had to go to a charity gala that night to represent Garvey Feinstein who couldn't make it, and that he sent a chauffeur to drive her there.

"What kind of a teenager car is that?" the puzzled boyfriend asked as he was looking out the window and seeing an oxblood-red car with small yellow flames drawn by the nicely rimmed wheels.

A worried Helda went to have a look at it, then said while trying to keep a placid tone and demeanor, "Oh, yes, it's his, uh, his new chauffeur. He's a kid, but he's a good driver. Very cautious, and respectful. Garvey told him to change the car."

Roy responded with a suspicious, slow nod.

"And do you really have to dress like that?" he followed.

"Dress like what?" a doe-eyed Helda asked.

Roy just stared at his girlfriend in response.

"I know it's a little risqué," Helda admitted. "But that's how most women will be dressed in that gala—you know Hollywood—so I'll blend in with the crowd. I'll be a dime a dozen. Most men will be there with their partners anyway. And I'll stick mostly with the girls."

The boyfriend paused for a second, then smiled, and said, "Okay... Sorry I distrusted you."

Helda said that it was okay. The couple kissed, and the assistant was out the door.

On her way to the car, Helda felt a rush of shame and discomfort at what she was doing. She didn't know why she was doing it. She felt like she was running on auto-pilot at that moment, like an invisible hand in the air was directing her and her actions. But the most conscious part of her reminded her that she was just being a good assistant, that that was what she had signed up for when she started working for the company. That was a good enough answer for her at the moment, enough to keep pushing her to the car with a bouncier step and a timid-but-excited smile.

As Helda was approaching the car, she overheard the two men yell, "Who's got swag?" and "I got swag!" which led her to mentally roll her eyes.

Justin saw the assistant and let the laid-down Garvey riding shotgun know. Garvey quickly instructed Justin to act professionally with Helda, as if he were her driver.

"Why?" Justin asked.

"Just do!" Garvey insisted.

So Justin hurried out of the car and opened the door to Helda by making a head nod that, from a distance, seemed to say, "Good evening, ma'am." What he actually said was a more predatory, "You look hot, ma'am. You're going to provoke a riot with this thing," most likely referring to her outfit.

Helda just got into the car with her head down and a contained smile.

Garvey turned around, took a look at his prettied-up assistant with above-knee-length tight dress and heels, and let out a genuine, "Damn," and Helda responded with a curt and dutiful, "Thank you."

After a moment of silence, she asked, "So, will anyone tell me where we're going?"

"I told you," Garvey answered. "To some venue in LA. It's called 'Area.'"

"Um, okay, you said that, to 'parade' me," said an apprehensive and irritable Helda while trying to show a neutral face and an even temper. "But what's the occasion?"

Garvey pointed his head to Justin and asked Helda, "You know who's Justin? And what he does?"

"I was hoping you'd tell me eventually," Helda replied.

"He's a pick-up artist," Garvey confessed as he looked his assistant straight in the eye.

"A pick-up artist…" Helda calmly reiterated as she opened her eyes wider.

"Pretend I'm not here," Justin interjected lightheartedly.

Garvey and Helda smiled briefly at the remark, then continued.

"He's just there to help me out with the chicks. I mean, you know better than anyone else how things can go wrong when I get in there headfirst with my usual ways," Garvey confided to the concurring nods of Helda. "If they didn't, you and San and Stuart wouldn't be there to pick up the pieces."

"Okay, that's fine," Helda conceded. "But what do you need to parade me for?"

As Garvey opened his mouth and before he said anything, his phone rang. An unknown number appeared.

"Hello," Garvey answered. "Oh, hi. (…) No problem, how can I help you? (…) Yeah, and I'm very grateful she's doing this tonight. I couldn't make it. (…) Uh, no later than 11 p.m., most likely. She should be home by midnight. (…) Alright. Alright, you're welcome. (…) No Problem. Bye."

It was Helda's boyfriend checking in on the event, and Garvey had the presence of mind to play along. Roy obtained Garvey's number by checking into his girlfriend's inbox on her computer where Garvey's professional number was attached to each of his emails.

When Garvey informed Helda of the call, the woman was shocked, as she didn't how he got the number. She felt embarrassed and apologized to Garvey. "I only gave him the number in case of extreme emergencies," she pleaded. But Garvey said it was okay and didn't really mind because he saw "embarrassed and contrite Helda" as an opportunity to get her to play along the preselection game more readily and willingly.

"So you asked about what you were going to do tonight?" Garvey reintroduced the topic.

"Yes!" Helda responded with dutiful enthusiasm. "So what will I do tonight?"

"Tonight, dear Helda, you'll be serving as arm candy," Garvey announced in a lecturing tone. "As my hot arm candy."

Helda cracked an embarrassed smile, then said with a raised eyebrow, "Your hot arm candy?" Justin was smiling too.

"Yes!" Garvey affirmed. "I want people to see this," he continued as he pointed with his hand and his ogling eyes at Helda's entirety, "and see me owning this, and go, 'Wow, I want to get with that Garvey guy, too!'" Then Garvey turned to Justin, and asked, "Is that what this preselection is about?"

"Pretty much," Justin casually replied.

Fifteen minutes later, Garvey was entering the club with his hand around Helda's waist, pulling her to him. His grab was rather forceful and touched the upper part of his assistant's buttocks.

Helda was a little discomforted at first by Garvey's grab, but then quickly made her peace with it as she was just glad someone was guiding her through that unusual venue and with so many people checking her up and down, even if surreptitiously. She felt visually assaulted by the attention on her and her body, which made Garvey's hand feel more protective than anything else at that moment.

Helda was following Garvey's lead, who was following Justin's, who had been in that establishment quite a few times before. According to Justin, *Area* was the perfect mix between "drunken partying and chill chatting," as it had a dancefloor and a bar on one side, and classy, more sober tables on the other.

"So here's how we're doing it," Justin instructed: "You parade your woman for a little while at the bar, ordering a drink, and I spot which of these chicks are checking you out with interest. And then when we all go to sit at the table, I'll refer you to the girls and you go open them, you know, like we did in the park. You can redo that, right?"

"Of course!" a cocksure Garvey asserted.

"And then you tell them, whatever, that she's just your assistant, just a girl you take care of, your sister... So long as they're interested in you, and you keep it cool, it's all good," Justin explained. "Sounds good?"

"Sounds great!" Garvey enthusiastically replied, before he and Helda headed to the bar.

Meanwhile, Roy was sitting in his car in front of the club seething with anger at his girlfriend's lie, and also at Garvey's. As soon he had hung up with the man moments earlier, Roy revved up his engine and began looking for the vehicle of the supposed chauffeur. Luckily for him, a teenager's ride with flames on the sides was easy to spot, so passersby were helpful in telling him where they saw it go.

The boyfriend got out of his car, went up to the bouncer, and asked him if there was a charity event inside. The bouncer said no with a chuckle. Roy turned around and headed back to his car in a determined gait and vacant gaze betraying both anger and sadness.

Meanwhile, Garvey was chatting up a woman at the bar who was pointed to by Justin, while trying to keep himself from bringing up his Hollywood credentials.

As he was hitting it off with the woman, Garvey received a text from Evelyn that said, "I loved your little speech from the heart the other day. You're cute when you're being yourself :) Miss you." He gave it a quick glance, then put his phone back in his pocket, and resumed his conversation with the young woman.

Garvey genuinely liked Evelyn, whom he saw as wife material, but this was not the time. At that particular moment, Garvey's sole concern was pulling off a pick-up without the crutch of his Hollywood status, and without incidents. Little did he know, something beyond his control was fomenting ten miles away, at Helda's place.

Indeed, Roy went back home, and the first thing he did after dropping his keys on the table was open his girlfriend's laptop again and log back into her inbox. For the following hour, he checked some eighty exchanges between her and Garvey, most of which were run-of-the-mill "postpone my appointment"-type memos.

In one of the incoming mails, Garvey told Helda to just ignore a certain man named Dorian and not respond to his calls or emails again, following three messages from Helda transmitting Dorian's new contact information and asking Garvey to get back in touch with him. In the last message involving Dorian, Helda informed Garvey of the following: "Dorian says he got your 'cowardly void message,' that he won't try to contact you for now, but that he'll never forget and that karma was a bitch." Garvey simply responded with, "lol." And that was the end from Dorian.

Roy's interest was piqued by this aggrieved fellow. So much so that he saved his phone number, not being sure what to do with it just yet. He wrote it on a piece of paper, and kept staring at that paper and cogitating about how to make use of it. "Hi! I'm the boyfriend of the assistant of the guy who won't return your calls?" he sarcastically suggested to himself.

But Roy was himself aggrieved with Garvey that he felt he might just have common cause with this man. So, he mustered up some courage, took ten seconds to think of the broad lines of what he would say to him, dialed his number on his phone, pressed "Call," then cancelled the call. "It's 11 p.m.," he thought to himself. "I'll call him tomorrow."

A half an hour later, Justin's car parked in front of the boyfriend's house, and Helda came out of it. Roy was watching TV in the living room. Helda entered and greeted her boyfriend with a smile and a seeming good mood, while Roy returned a less enthusiastic, "Hi."

"So how was the gala?" he asked.

"Great, great," she replied as she was taking off her earrings. "We raised a lot of money for the cancer kids. It was truly heartwarming."

"Uh-uh," Roy responded incredulously. "And how much did you raise?"

"I think it was ten million…"

"We're over," Roy abruptly announced.

"What?!" the shocked girlfriend exclaimed.

"I know you didn't go to a charity gala," Roy stated with a plain intonation, before laying out the rest of his case with the same cool, knowing tone. "I know that kid wasn't your chauffeur—what kind of chauffeur goes around in a sports car? And what kind of chauffeur spends the night in the venue he was supposed to just drive his client to?—I know Feinstein was there with you. I don't know why you lied about the gala, about Feinstein going there, about the kid with the sport car. And I don't want to know. You've lied way too much for it to matter. So, this is over."

Helda stood there mouth agape and for a few seconds, before breaking her silence in a weak voice, "Please let me explain."

"I said it's over, Helda," Roy pronounced as he stood up and faced the woman with an unflinching stare. "Here's your money for this month's rent. I appreciate you insisting on contributing to live here. You can stay here two more weeks as a roommate, without the rent. For old times' sake. And also because I snooped into your emails."

Roy pointed to her room with his hand. Helda stood there in disbelief for a while, attempting to process what had just happened in the span of a minute. She had never seen Roy act this cold and unyielding in the nine months she had been with him. But the deep sense of betrayal turned the 34-year-old man into an unfeeling payback machine, especially that this was just one more episode in a string of his girlfriend's lies—the one that broke the proverbial camel's back. The woman, overwhelmed, just turned around and headed to her room while trying to contain her tears midway.

As Helda shut the door to her room, Roy sighed, then said, "On to Feinstein now."

When it came to Garvey, Roy didn't know where to start. But he knew there was a person from his past who most likely still held some resentment towards the Hollywood hotshot, and that person might have some compromising information on the man. As Roy had it in mind, Dorian would hopefully share that information, and Roy would either render it public, share it to the press, or encourage the disgruntled wannabe filmmaker to do so. So, the next day, Roy dialed the man's number, and waited for someone to answer.

"Hello?" a young man's voice said.

"Hi," Roy greeted back. "Is this Dorian?"

"This is him," Dorian answered. "Who am I speaking to?"

"I am, uh– I am an employee of Garvey Feinstein," said Roy as he was trying to recollect his thoughts. "This is…"

"Oh," Dorian uttered.

"I know," Roy said understandingly. "I know this may sound out of the blue, but I was the person who received your calls and messages to Mr. Feinstein. And the reason you didn't get responses from them is simply that he didn't want to have anything to do with you. And to be honest, I was pained by what I had to do, but I had to, as part of my job."

"Okay…"

"And so… I guess this is a belated apology from me, now that I don't work for Feinstein anymore," Roy confided.

"Well, that's– that was unexpected," said a visibly surprised Dorian as he let out a little laugh. "Thank you, I guess. Did you just get fired, or--?"

"Well, yes, last week. But you know, I was going through the mails and– and now that I'm sort of in your shoes, I understand it must've hurt to be dropped so unceremoniously by Garvey," Roy intimated.

"Well…" Dorian replied, still with a hint of speechlessness in his voice and words. "Thank you. Thanks for your understanding. And, yeah, I guess it did hurt. But you know what, I've moved on. It's been a while now. And the guy is just weird. No offense."

"None taken," quickly retorted Roy. "You're referring to Garvey, right?"

"Yeah."

"And… Like, what do you mean 'weird'?" Roy asked as he tried to keep himself from sounding too eager in his questioning. "You mean… Because I never really noticed."

"It's just the way he talks in general," Dorian said. "He can come off as awkward, sometimes too pushy or needy. He probably wasn't needy towards you because he was your boss. But that's just how he came off to me. In addition to the little things."

"The little things?"

"Yeah, you know, like-- like his Skype handle, it was 'VelvetEglantine24'!" Dorian gushed. "And it was so incongruent with a guy like Garvey, physically and otherwise. I mean, the last thing that comes to your mind when you think of him is a velvet eglantine. You know what I mean?"

"I do, I do…" responded a smiling Roy as he was taking notes. "Yeah, that's Feinstein for ya!"

The two temporarily-allied men chatted for two more minutes, with Dorian sharing one more anecdote, and Roy delightedly taking a few more notes. Roy then thanked him, wished him good luck, and the men ended their conversation there.

As Roy hung up, he stared at his little piece of paper containing juicy Feinstein-related information with a grin on his face. He just sat there one full minute reflecting on what to do with it, then headed to his laptop, and searched "velveteglatine24 skype."

Roy wanted to first make sure that profile existed. That search failed to turn up any Skype-related results, so Roy realized he had to look for it within the application. As he was about to write "download skype," his eyes caught a couple of results from the former search containing profiles with the exact username "velveteglantine24" making comments on various forums.

"What are the odds?" Roy thought to himself out loud. "Not just 'eglantine,' which is in itself rare, *velvet* eglantine... and twenty-four!"

Roy realized it was almost certainly Garvey behind that highly specific username. His heart started beating with excitement.

"Let's look at what this schmuck's going around the internet sharing," Roy thought.

The vexed boyfriend scrolled down the list of results, until one from a website called *darkdesires.com* caught his attention. "Oh, we've got a real perv over here!"

Roy avidly clicked on that page. And a series of posts on rape fantasies appeared, one of which was made by member *VelvetEglantine24* titled, "Coming Clean ..."

A flabbergasted Roy read the entirety of the post, which was basically an admission of rape.

"You nasty degenerate!" the disgruntled man commented, before he wondered why hadn't anyone on that forum reported him. Though, after he saw Garvey's mention in his post that he was using an IP spoofer, he figured that was probably why the other members didn't bother, especially that there were a few other "confessions" of rape on that forum as well.

But Roy knew that this was Garvey behind the screen, and no amount of IP spoofing could hide that. As such, the nosy, vindictive former boyfriend dialed 911.

"Nine-one-one, what is your emergency?" a woman responded.

"Hi," said an anxious-but-excited Roy. "So, uh, I think I just came across an admission of rape by a person I know. They wrote it online... That they did it."

"Okay," the interlocutor said. "I will give you an email address, and you could send me the link to that rape admission along with the relevant information you have about the person, and I will forward it to the police."

"Yeah, uh… The thing is, he probably hid his IP address, and you won't able to track him," Roy informed the operator.

"Then how do you know it's him?" she asked.

"Because the username of that profile is the exact same one as that man's Skype profile," Roy asserted. "And it's very, very specific."

"Okay, okay," said the operator in an interested and focused voice. "An online confession of rape is definitely grounds for a police investigation and possible arrest and prosecution. So you did the right thing."

"Uh-huh…" said Roy as he was cracking a smile upon hearing this.

"So, what I would like you to do is go to the nearest police station, and inform the officers there of the Internet post and every other relevant information about the person you believe posted it," the operator instructed. "If you can't get to the station, I could call for some officers from there to come by your home and have a chat with you."

"No, no, that's fine," Roy answered. "I'll go there myself and explain it all to them."

"Perfect," the operator rejoined. "If you need any more information, call 911 again—extension 629 if you wish to get to me specifically. I'm available Mondays through Thursdays, 6 a.m. to 2 p.m. Pacific."

"Thanks a lot, ma'am!" Roy said appreciatively. "You've been helpful. Goodbye."

"Bye."

Roy hung up, blew a powerful sigh of relief and excitement, then went to get himself ready.

Five minutes later, he was out the door. A minute after that, he came back in a hurry, and found Helda in the living room. They both exchanged polite and awkward "hi"s. Helda had a day off that day, but Roy was in too much of a mental rush to wonder why she was locking herself in her room the entire morning or why her eyes were red.

Roy had come back for his laptop. He wanted to check the link to that forum so he could give it directly to the officers. He wrote it on a piece of paper, along with Garvey's username, and was out of the door in less than two minutes.

A short while later, Roy was entering the police station with a scrap of paper and a racing heart.

"Hello," he said to the first officer he encountered. "I'd like to report a crime."

"Okay, Sir. Have a seat," replied the mustached man as he pointed to an empty chair next to his desk. "I'll be right with you."

Roy said, "Alright," then went to have a seat. The officer came back three minutes later.

"Okay!" the policeman exclaimed as an introduction to their conversation as he sat down. "I'm officer Calieri. What seems to be the crime?"

"Hi," Roy said. "I'm Roy Corke. So… I sort of saw a confession of rape on the Internet."

"Okay…" said the officer in a tone that suggested, "Go on."

"A person, a man, under the alias *VelvetEglantine24* wrote an account in which he forced himself on a woman, while specifying that the story was true," Roy reported.

"Uh-huh," uttered the officer as he was taking notes. "And do you have an idea who that person might be?"

"As a matter of fact, I do," Roy answered. "I think he might be my ex-girlfriend's boss, Garvey Feinstein."

"Hmm, Garvey Feinstein…" Officer Calieri said pensively. "I've heard of that name before."

"He's a Hollywood producer," Roy informed the officer.

"Right, right. Yeah, I see who it is." Calieri said. "And so, how do you know it's him?"

Roy then went on to mention the eerily similar Skype username and Garvey's questionable reputation with women. The officer listened with interest, then, when Roy was done, said, "Gotcha!" and grabbed the phone in a very purposeful manner.

"Hey, is Luke around?" the officer asked on the phone. "Right. Send him in, please. And tell him to bring his laptop," before curtly hanging up.

Luke was a computer specialist who worked with the police.

"Looks like we have some IP tracking to do," Calieri said as he sat back and crossed his two hands on his stomach.

In the meantime, the two men talked some more about Garvey and how Roy knew him. Roy tried to polish the truth for a while, saying he had worked under Feinstein and had obtained his Skype directly from him, but then saw no point in clinging to those little lies that would just hurt his credibility further when discovered. So, he laid it all as it happened: his prying into his ex-girlfriend's emails due to the jealousy, him being motivated by revenge, calling Dorian, and obtaining all of that information from him, with the officer taking the occasional notes, until the slim-figured IT whizz arrived.

"Hey, there!" Luke greeted the two men.

"Hey, Luke," Officer Calieri said, before introducing him to Roy. "This is Luke Bahmer, our very talented IT guy."

The two men shook hands and said, "Nice to meet you."

"So what are we having today?" Luke asked hungrily as he opened his laptop.

"A rape story, I'm afraid," the officer responded casually with his raspy voice before pulling a cigarette out of his shirt pocket.

"Okay, then!"

"Some guy confessed to forcing himself on a woman on an online forum, and specified it was a true story," the officer continued before turning to Roy and asking, "Is that about right?"

"That's about it," Roy concurred, before handing a piece of paper to Luke and saying, "Here's the link to that page. I archived it on the Wayback Machine in case it's not there anymore."

"You did the right thing," Luke commented with a quick, casual wink as he was entering the address.

"We want you to track the user's IP address," Calieri instructed. "Can you do that?"

"I sure can!" Luke retorted with the same cheerful attitude. "Unless he hid his ass."

"He hid his what?" Roy asked.

"Hide My Ass," Luke explained. "It's a VPN service to browse the internet anonymously."

Roy remembered reading Garvey's mention of him hiding his traces, but he kept it to himself at that moment because he didn't want to dampen Luke's enthusiasm when it was at its height a minute earlier.

"Oh, no!" Roy exclaimed five seconds upon Luke arriving to Garvey's text. "Look, he said he hid his ass!"

"Where?" Luke asked.

"Here!" Roy pointed somewhere in the text.

"Oh, yeah," Luke reacted. "Well, that sucks. Let's check it out."

Luke then attempted to track the IP of that profile, but to no avail. "Looks like he did hide his ass," he commented.

"Do you have any other online information about the man?" Luke asked as he looked to the officer.

"Yeah, we have his Skype handle," Calieri responded with a smoke in his hand.

Luke accessed Skype, did his IT tricks, but then said, "I can't get his IP like that. Though I could get it from a conversation with him."

The officer started to get impatient, and told Luke, "Give me that phone. We're not going to wait an eternity to have a chit-chat with the guy!"

The officer dialed 411, then asked whoever picked to put him through anyone from Skype. The operator did.

"Hi, this is Officer Calieri from the LAPD," the policeman introduced himself. "I'd like to talk to someone higher up in the corporate ladder about an ongoing investigation."

"Uh, okay," the Skype operator said, seemingly caught off-guard. "Please hold on a second."

Three minutes later, a man picked up:

"Hello, this is Enrique Nesedo, head of Business Development. How may I help you?" he said in a friendly voice.

"Hi, I'm Officer Dean Calieri from the LAPD," the officer said. "We have suspicions that one of your users has been involved in a crime—namely, a rape—and we'd like to track his IP. Can you do that for us?"

"Umm, I believe we can," the man answered. "But I'm going to need to see some identification on your part, please."

"Why not just check the number I'm calling you from; It's the LAPD's," the officer noted in a somewhat snarky tone.

"Okay, one moment, please," Enrique said.

The officer rolled his eyes. Meanwhile, Enrique called the directory assistance and asked where that number was from. Once they confirmed it was from the police station, he asked the officer to give him Garvey's username, then charged one of his underlings to track their user's IPs.

Calieri thanked him, and Enrique asked the policeman to leave an email address to which he would be sending him all relevant information shortly. The officer did, and the conversation ended there.

"Now, what?" Roy asked.

"Now, we wait," Calieri replied. "We wait for their email."

The three men just sat there for a while. Roy didn't know what to break the awkward silence with, so he asked the officer for a smoke, and Calieri obliged. Roy lit it up, inhaled a deep breath, then effused, "Oh, yeah, that feels good."

"I'm trying to quit," Dean casually remarked as he was about to finish his own.

"Good call," Roy commented.

The two men were bobbing their heads while Luke was playing with his phone when the officer's screen signaled one incoming email. It was a mail from Skype's Head of Business Development himself, and contained a long list of VelvetEglantine24's logins on the application, with the times, dates, browsers, and, most importantly, the IP addresses of each login.

Dean sent a quick reply to Enrique, thanking him and his company for their cooperation. He then slapped and rubbed his hands, and enthused, "Let's get to business!" and continued, "Okay. So let's the start with the most common IP we've got here. Looks like it's this one, right?"

Roy and Luke looked at the screen, then confirmed, "Yeah."

"Right. Now, Luke, you tell me where this IP bad boy is from!"

Luke went back to his laptop, did some research, and less than one minute later, he announced, "It's around Santa Monica."

Roy and the policeman looked at each other, and Roy said, "That's where he works. His office's on Olympic Boulevard."

Dean turned to Luke and asked him if that address could be from there, and Luke's answer was, "Very likely."

"What do you mean?" Dean asked.

"I mean 'very likely,'" Luke replied. "If your guy is from there, then yeah, that's his IP. The only thing I'm one-hundred percent sure of is that it's from the area, from LA. But this particular one comes most often from Santa Monica."

The three men sat pondering on what to do next. Luke asked whether he was needed any longer, then excused himself. As to Roy and Officer Calieri, they sat there and had a little back-and-forth on how likely it was for two different people to have this specific a screen name.

"Hey, Mike!" Dean called his colleague out from his desk. "Tell me, if you saw some profile called *VelvetEglantine24* on some website, and then you went on to another website and saw that exact same profile, too, you'd assume it's the same person, right?"

Mike paused for a few seconds while making a DeNiro face, then said, "Yeah... I mean, most people don't even know what 'eglantine' is, let alone attach a color and a number to it. Yeah, I'd say it's the same person, 95 percent chance."

Dean bobbed his head, thanked Mike, then slapped his hands together, and announced, "Alright, that settles it: we're investigating the creep!"

Roy cracked an approving smile while bobbing his head as well.

"Let me take the case to the captain first," Dean said as he stood up and headed for an office in that precinct.

Calieri came back from the captain's office a few minutes later. He was assigned a colleague of his to work the case with him.

"Roy, this is Officer Flanagan. She'll be working the case with me," Dean announced.

Roy said hi with a smile, and shook hands with Debra, the policewoman, who did the same.

Debra began by noting that the account *VelvetEglantine24* gave strongly implied he had known the woman before the incident, well enough that she let him in her home, where he did it.

"I understand your girlfriend has been working for him for a while now, and knows him?" she asked.

"She has," Roy replied. "But it's not her. If we go by that post, this happened in the woman's home, and Helda's home was *my* home for the past year. Plus, if something this traumatic had happened to her, it would've surfaced somehow and affected her behavior. To my knowledge, it didn't. She was never… 'shook' or anything. Sometimes down or unstable, but not unlike other women I'd dated."

The two officers slightly smiled at that last remark.

"Be that as it may," Officer Flanagan initiated her response with a hint of a smile still on her face, "she's still of interest to us because she likely knows the women Garvey has been with and around."

Roy nodded.

"How many years has she been working for Feinstein now?" she asked.

"I think two," Roy replied. "Two years, maybe a little more."

Debra said, "Right…" then remained silent. That's when Dean interjected, asked Roy for his ex-girlfriend's full name and the address where she was staying. Roy imparted the necessary information, and the two officers were on their way.

"You're coming along with us to your place?" Dean asked.

"No, that's fine. I'll come home later on. I'll let you three alone," Roy answered. "If you need any more information about the case, don't hesitate to call me, anytime."

"Alright," Dean said. "And you too if you remember anything that might help us."

Roy said he would, then left the police station.

The officers, on their part, were on their way to his house. And fifteen minutes later, they were knocking on his door.

A surprised Helda opened, and asked if she could help them. Officer Flanagan told her they wanted to ask her a few questions about her boss. Helda said, "Okay," and let them in.

"So Friday's off for you?" Dean asked as they were taking a seat in the living room.

"My boss had me working long hours yesterday, so he gave me this morning off." Helda said.

"What were you working on?"

"Garvey's social skills," Helda answered as she let out an uncomfortable chuckle.

"Care to develop a little on that?" Dean asked.

Helda sighed then said, "We went out to some venue downtown so that Mr. Feinstein could pick up a woman, under the supervision of a 'pick-up artist.'"

"A pick-up artist?" Debra asked.

"Yes, he hired this kid to help make his interactions and approaches of women go 'smoother,'" she replied by using airquotes again.

"Sounds like Feinstein's interactions with the opposite sex are often tumultuous," Dean noted.

The officers then asked some more about Garvey's said interactions and relations with the women around him, and Helda reluctantly answered. She didn't want Garvey to know she had been telling on him to the police. Dean sensed that when he saw her look away and scratch her face while answering, so he reassured her that Feinstein would never find out about who told them this information, or if they knew about it at all. "We're just trying to put the pieces of the puzzle for now," he said.

"What if it ends up in court and all of this is used against him?" she asked, worried. "Or if I'm called to testify right in front of him?"

"Okay, he's your boss, but he's not a mobster," Dean reassured. "He'd just fire you, at worst, not put a hit on you. And if he ends up in court, then, well, your testimony will have helped bring down a sexual predator. And your cooperation will be seen as heroic rather than treacherous." Dean then switched to a warmer and more paternalistic tone, and said while putting his hand reassuringly on her knee, "If it ever comes down to that, a hero like yourself will be rehired elsewhere, trust me."

A more-reassured-but-still-wary Helda nodded, then asked, "So is that what he did? You think he sexually assaulted someone?"

"Yes," Dean replied with the same warm tone. "We have reason to believe he did, but we can't tell you more about it now. How you could help, though, is by telling us the names of the women Feinstein was around the most lately, women he was possibly intimate with."

At that moment, Dean's phone rang.

"Calieri," he answered. "Oh, yeah? (…) Uh-huh. (…) Right. (…) Okay, thanks."

Dean wrote down a quick note during the conversation, then asked Helda to go ahead and answer his question. Helda told the officers that Garvey often tried to get with the actresses they auditioned, and that, to her knowledge, the last two he had been with were Ellen Chen and Evelyn West.

"There ya go!" Dean exclaimed as he cheerfully pointed his finger at Helda.

"What?" Debra asked.

"This was the sergeant on the phone," Dean said. "He told us Garvey Feinstein was arrested a while ago for attempted sexual assault of a woman named Evelyn West. The charges were eventually dropped."

"That's our woman," Debra noted.

The officers thanked Helda for her cooperation, and, less than thirty minutes later, they were knocking on Evelyn's door. Nobody was there, so they waited in their car for an hour, until Evelyn came in. They gave her ten more minutes to wash and wind down, then were knocking on her door again.

After the introduction and the usual surprise on the woman's part, she let them in, and they were on her couch. Officer Calieri told her it was about Garvey Feinstein, then, within the same minute, cut to the chase: "Did he do anything in your presence, or knowledge, that could be viewed as criminal?"

Evelyn was taken aback by the question. "Uhh… What kind of thing?" she asked.

Dean saw Evelyn's mild state of shock, so he decided to go about it more diplomatically.

"I don't know," he said. "Perhaps something of a sexual nature?"

"I... I... No, not to my recollection," Evelyn answered.

Dean and Debra looked at each other, then Dean extended his hand to his partner as he gave her a complicit look. This prompted Debra to pull out a folded piece of paper from a pocket of hers and give it to Dean, who then handed it to Evelyn, saying, "Read this, and tell us if it reminds you of something."

Evelyn unfolded the piece of paper and started reading. Ten seconds into it, she began to visibly flinch and cringe.

In the meantime, Roy was on his way back home. When he arrived and opened the door, he saw his ex-girlfriend sitting there, visibly distraught. The man quickly understood the two police officers did pay her a visit.

Roy dropped his keys on a stand near the entrance, and, in a dry tone said, "What's up?"

"Nothing," Helda replied.

A moment of silence ensued, then, as Roy went to wash, he said, "I heard the police came by."

Helda's eyes opened in surprise.

"Who told you that?" she asked.

"Neighbors," he answered.

"Mr. Klein?"

"Not important," Roy said before he came out of the bathroom with a towel drying up his hands. "So what did they want?"

"Oh, they were just looking for witnesses about a robbery that happened nearby," Helda said.

Roy finished drying himself up, looked at Helda with something of a smirk and mischievously raised eyebrow, and asked, "Was the name of the robber... Garvey?"

Helda looked at Roy nervously for a few seconds, then, all emotional, concluded, "Oh, my God! You were behind this! You're sending the cops after Feinstein!"

"I'm sending the cops after a likely sex offender," Roy rejoined.

Helda looked down in exasperation, sat silently for a few seconds, then asked, "Why are you doing this?"

"Why did you cheat on me with Garvey?" Roy countered curtly.

"I didn't!"

"You did!" he insisted loudly while pointing a finger. "I saw you getting in that club with him that night! And I don't want to hear it anymore!"

Helda sighed, and said, "If you don't want to hear it, then what do you want from me? And why are you coming after him?"

"Payback," Roy replied. "You wronged me, I wrong you. The both of you. I'm making sure the guy gets at least harassed by the cops for a while. And you I'm dumping and throwing out for it."

Helda glanced at Roy furtively, then looked down, feeling both offended and strangely turned on by his unyielding resolve and hardheaded assertions.

"And does that make you happy?" she asked.

"A little," he said in a calmer tone as he casually leaned against the stand. "Though, to be completely honest, I don't like seeing you go away. But you have to atone for your bad deeds, for screwing me over."

"I do," Helda agreed somewhat enthusiastically. "But it doesn't have to be you kicking me out, ending what we have between us!"

Roy stared at his ex for a while then contemplatively said, "It doesn't..." while approaching her in slow but determined steps until he stood ten inches from her. Suddenly, he grabbed her arm, pulled her up, sat on the couch's arm, and laid her on his lap like a little girl. Helda asked what he was doing, but Roy only slapped her contemptuously in response. He then proceeded to pull down her pants and began slapping her buttocks hard enough for the sound of the smack to reverberate throughout the room. Five smacks in, and the woman already started to tear up. She felt small, and flinched and blinked at each hit while hearing admonitions of the sort of, "I can't believe I've had a slut for a girlfriend all this time!" and "I provided her a home and a structure while she was whoring herself to her boss" along with the spanks.

At that exact moment, Evelyn was blinking at Garvey's lurid account, flinching in the same manner, just as if she were being spanked by Garvey's colorful words, which were hitting too close to home. And how could they not? It was her. And she relived every little feeling she had lived that night as she was perusing those words. Those feelings were mixed, conflicting, and definitely overwhelming. So much so that her eyes began watering as well halfway through the letter.

When she couldn't hold her tears, the two officers gave each other a self-satisfied look that said, "We got her."

Debra approached the aggrieved, weeping woman, and tapped on her shoulder in consolation.

"It's okay, it's okay," she said. "We'll get him. We'll get him for you."

"For me?" Evelyn wondered as she wiped her tears. "Garvey didn't do anything to me!"

The two officers looked at her with a raised eyebrow, then Dean asked incredulously, "Why are you crying then?"

"It's just sad, that's all," Evelyn responded. "I just feel bad for the woman."

"Right..." Dean commented with the same incredulous tone. "So this doesn't bring up anything at all? Is that what you're saying?"

"Yes!" Evelyn said while trying to keep a poker face.

The two officers left it there, then left her home, but not without some long "we're not sure we're believing you" stares.

Evelyn wasn't so sure why she opted to protect Garvey, the man who raped her. A part of her simply didn't want to rock the boat—an arrest might have led to an indictment, which might have led to the whole movie getting canceled. It would have been foolish for her to ruin her big break like that. Or so she kept rationalizing her decision after the police officers left.

"Yeah!" she thought to herself. "Why would I jeopardize my entire career for something I can still do later on?"

To her mind, she could still report everything once the movie gets done. That way, the actors and all the participants in it wouldn't suffer, and Garvey would still get his due eventually.

Yet, a part of Evelyn knew that a big reason behind her indecisiveness was that she was still unsure about how to feel about what happened. She knew that, technically and legally, it was an evil act of rape. But a part of her was still hoping it was more of a vigorous prelude to something great, to something great with her and Garvey, the man who forced himself into her life. Thus, Evelyn's sentiments about that infamous night would eventually depend on what Garvey was about to make of it: either a troubled beginning of something great, an actual conquest of the woman he lusted after and hopefully loved; or a lowly act of abuse of a man merely looking for a vessel to relieve himself with.

As such, Garvey's coming actions proved not only fateful for Evelyn and her perception of what had happened, but also for the producer's career, future, reputation, and life, which all became in the hands of the one woman.

* * * *

It had been almost a week since Garvey gave any sign to Evelyn, who was feeling increasingly hurt by it. So she decided to give the man a final 48 hours before making any decision. But for Garvey, old habits died hard, and he was well on his way to pull another "Dorian" on the woman he auditioned then raped. Except that the Dorians of the world don't take this kind of pump-and-dump too fondly.

Two days later, the phone of Officer Flanagan rang.

"It was me," Evelyn solemnly announced. "It was me on that account."

Debra showed the beginning of a smile in response, and twenty minutes later, she and Dean were on Evelyn's doorstep.

They were let in, and Evelyn told them the whole story, from the audition, to the meeting with Moody Alan, to the incident in the hotel room, and to her personal and violent entanglement with the man. The officers recorded the entire conversation on tape, then went to Ellen's, and did the same with her testimony. Ellen hesitated at first because she had taken the hush money, but the officers convinced her that money only meant she wouldn't report Garvey herself, not that she should hide valuable, crime-related information from the police, and that it would make her an accomplice if she did.

Later that day, Garvey was in the studio talking to a young woman.

"And so," he intimated, "you're going to need a little more than talent to become a full-blown actress. I mean, don't get me wrong, you do have the talent. But, at the end of the day, this is a network, and so, you've gotta network, get into the good graces of the gatekeepers, you follow me?"

Garvey then excused himself to the bathroom, and asked the young woman to wait for him in his office in the meantime.

In there, he grabbed his phone and began texting his pick-up artist: "Dude, she's giving me IOIs, looks totally DTF. Should I move on her RIGHT NOW?" Two minutes later, Justin texted back, "Absolutely. Go ahead and don't overthink it. You Got Swag!"

Garvey felt charged up by that text. He tucked his phone back in, aggressively nodded his head as if he had just set out on a mission, and kept on repeating, "I got swag!" as he was headed out of the restroom.

"I got swag. That swag, I got it!" he affirmed as he was about to open the bathroom door. "See this swag? It's mine! I've g…"

"You've got pending criminal charges," curtly quipped a man in uniform facing Garvey as he opened the door. That man was Officer Calieri. "Cuff him up," he ordered.

Garvey stood frozen in response. He tried to keep an inexpressive face, but his heart was racing.

"This is ridiculous," he said as he was being handcuffed.

"You have the right to remain silent," Dean said in response while they were taking Garvey to the police car with everyone standing and watching in the hallway. "Anything you say can and will be used against you in a court of law…"

"Yeah, yeah."

"You have the right to an attorney. If you can't afford one, …"

"I made $4M on my last movie, fucko."

"… one will be appointed to you by the court. With these rights in mind, are you still willing to talk to me about the charges against you?"

"And what charges would those be?" Garvey asked with a defiant, devil-may-care attitude.

"Second-degree sexual assault… fucko," Dean replied.

As Garvey was dragged through the hall, he saw almost every one of his colleagues and subordinates standing there, watching the scene unfold in shock, though not in entire disbelief. One of those standing there was his assistant Sanjeep. As Garvey passed by her, he said, "Tell Stuart to call me."

The man was taken to the station, interrogated, charged, then let out on an $800,000 bail. His trial was scheduled two months from then.

Garvey returned home despondent, looking and feeling like a defeated man, which he was—his lawyer made it clear to him that his defenses were limited, and that the prosecution had a solid case against him.

He threw himself on his couch, a bottle of scotch in one hand, his phone in the other. He took a gulp of whiskey, then typed and sent, "Why?" Three minutes later, he received, "You dug your own grave" from Evelyn. Garvey felt even more despondent upon reading that, and didn't have the mental fortitude to respond to it, partly because that sentence rang very true in his head.

Hammering the final nail was the ad-hoc board-of-directors meeting the following day, wherein Feinstein was convened then unanimously fired from his own company.

The former Hollywood producer spent the two months that followed in his home, isolated from society. He had convinced a teenage neighbor of his to discreetly drop by his house every five days, to be given a list of things to buy for Garvey, and then be repaid 150 percent of whatever he bought. But, besides that, he had little human contact, except for the few times he went out at night to see Almóndolar, and Taki, an old Greek friend of his.

Three weeks in, he was sitting in his armchair watching TV, a story about actor Marvin Slicey allegedly coming on to a male minor. Garvey couldn't go online anymore, as the vitriol in it about him only weighed him down further.

Some evening, at nine o'clock, the door rang. Garvey dragged himself to it and opened. It was Helda. As he opened, Helda was faced with a shell of a man. A stinky shell of a man in a raggedy bathrobe, an unkempt beard, and a strong body odor coupled with that of liquor.

"Hey," Garvey said in his deep, raspy voice which was only made raspier from the alcohol and the depression.

The man looked to Helda as if he had been living behind some obscure dumpster for the past three weeks. She was overwhelmed by the sight and the smell, but tried to remain placid, so she put on her most compassionate face, and said:

"Hi! How are you?"

"Doing great!" he said dispassionately as he dawdled back to his armchair.

"You don't look great," a diffident Helda noted as she closed the door and tentatively advanced towards the couch next to Garvey. "Did you get out at all since… you know?"

"Yeah, I couple of times," Garvey answered with the same morose, careless tone as he was staring into the void, liquor in hand.

"Like this?" Helda asked, referring to his appearance.

A rough, drawn, and haggard Garvey then turned to his former assistant, and asked, "What do you care?" He then started drawing nearer and nearer to her, only to repeat, "What do *you* care?"

Helda felt an intense grasp in her stomach as a beastlier-than-usual Garvey drew near her, with his shaggy, fuzzy facial hair and powerful reek, but froze in her place. She mustered just enough spirit to meekly answer, "Just checking," only for Garvey to retort, "I thought so" before he went to sit back on his armchair.

Helda may have been somewhat impressed and overwhelmed by Garvey's rough exterior, but at the end of the day, she knew she felt more pity for him than anything else.

At that moment, a barely recognizable Garvey began rubbing his crotch from atop his dirty bathrobe, then started groaning.

Helda just sat there with her eyes wide open watching Garvey falling back into his antics again. It wasn't his first time, but it was inappropriate and shocking enough that the aging man still had the juice to go there even in the worst of times.

Garvey rubbed himself while being aroused by Helda's mere presence. As he was getting harder and bigger, he grabbed the woman's hand, put it on his member, and rubbed it with his hand, as if to instruct her to keep stroking.

The man was so pathetic in the eyes of Helda, so dirty, down and out, low... that she got turned on as well. That pathetic loser was strangely sexy to her. So, she began stroking above his sweater pants. She then pulled down Garvey's pants and pulled his member, and began stroking it even harder, feeling it swell and stiffen in her hand. Garvey just raised his head and laid it on the top of the armchair, and began groaning. He had the appearance of a dying man, and, at that moment, also made the sounds of one.

Two minutes in, his grunts became more intense, until he shot up all over Helda's hand, then sighed in relief in his usual voice.

Helda looked around her, but didn't find any tissue. So she just went to the bathroom, rinsed her hand, dried it with a damp towel, then just headed from the bathroom straight to the door, and left. No word was uttered, from her or from Garvey, who just kept his head blissfully leaned on the head of the chair.

* * * *

Over a month passed, and Garvey was in a suit in a courthouse. The prosecution was pummeling the judge and jury with accounts from internet forums, with testimonies from Evelyn, Ellen, Helda, Sanjeep, and three other women, all of which pointed to one thing: Garvey Feinstein was a sexual predator.

Garvey felt especially betrayed by Helda's unfiltered admissions. He expected more loyalty on her part; after all, she did give him a half-hearted handjob that crummy night. He was all the more appalled when the woman spilled the beans about his cynical baseball assignments to the people around him, and so was the jury, all under the schadenfreude-ned eyes of Roy and Dorian who were assisting the trial.

Those two men's newfound affinity on the phone a couple of months earlier only strengthened when they had finally met in person

25 minutes before the trial. As Roy was seated on a bench outside the courtroom next to Helda, a young man approached him and asked when the trial of Garvey Feinstein was set to begin. Roy informed him it should begin at one o'clock. So the young man just sat next to him waiting.

"Are you a relative to one of Feinstein's victims?" the long-haired young man asked with a compassionate tone.

Roy glanced quickly at his again-girlfriend Helda because he realized he was referring to her, then said after a pause, "Sort of. Are you?"

"Sort of," the young man replied before he laid his hand and said, "I'm Dorian."

"Roy," said Roy as the two men shook hands. "Wait a second..."

Roy asked Dorian if he was the man he talked to on the phone, and Dorian said he was. "No way!" The vengeful boyfriend then came clean on the true motives of his phone call to Dorian as well as on the fact that he had never worked for Garvey. "So, in a sense, I was sort of impersonating her," referring to Helda, who was putting on a smile of a woman looking at a mischievous man, a smile that said, "That was pretty bad, but also cool enough that I might forgive you."

"Well, I forgive you," Dorian said to Roy. "I mean, you're the guy who set in motion this whole thing against that freak. And this far outweighs whatever fib you told me."

The two men looked each other fondly for a few seconds, then Dorian snapped out of it and suggested to the couple, "Hey, we still have some twenty minutes before the trial. What do you say we go grab a coffee or something? There's a joint on the side of this courthouse. On me."

Roy and Helda gladly accepted.

In the fast-food shop, Helda's seat gave her a glimpse on the courthouse entrance. And as the two men were eating sandwiches and talking, Helda just sat in silence watching the people coming into the court. Among those entering, she saw Sanjeep, Almóndolar, Moody Alan, and even pick-up artist Justin, who caught her attention with his suit and tie combined with one of his wild, weird, gelled-up hairdos and a feather sticking out of his vest.

Helda looked at all those people coming in with fondness, fondness for a simpler time that wouldn't be coming back. A part of her wished none of this had happened, and that things kept going at the production business as usual, with her as Garvey's assistant and "catcher." But the more rational part of her knew that Garvey had to be stopped, that he had it coming, and that this was the right course of action.

Helda was roused out of her dreamy stare towards the door by Roy asking her whether she wanted some coffee because he was going to order some for himself. She said no, and then went back to thinking: "Oh, well. I still have Roy, and get to live in his house rent-free."

The trio then headed back to court to watch the proceedings, and, in Helda's case, serve as witness as well.

Feinstein's defense relied mostly on the seeming willingness and consent of the various actresses and assistants. Stuart Aaronsohn's argument was that everyone who witnessed his client's interactions with those women never reported any form of coercion or blackmail, and that the women seemed to go along willingly and without showing any outward sign of distress.

The prosecutor, on the other hand, countered that the coercion was implied, and that, as the person with the final say on whether these women would get the role, or keep their job, the defendant wouldn't have had to be explicit and overt in order to exert a reasonable degree of coercion on his victims. The man then went on to mention the bathroom incident by calling Brad—the restaurant employee—to the stand, as an example of Garvey's coercive ways even with the women who were willingly with him.

"Furthermore," the prosecutor argued, "his demeaning and dehumanizing attitude and language when dealing with the women around him suggest he saw them as less than actual persons, and more as possessions, conquests, and acquisitions. To further expound on this, I would like to call Ms. Helda Jenkins to the stand."

The judge okayed the request with a nod, and Helda rose to the stand.

"Ms. Jenkins," the prosecutor opened, "could you first tell us briefly about your occupation within MaxiMir and the duration of your employment there?"

"I assisted Mr. Feinstein in his daily dealings with the people who wanted to see him or had done business with him. I played the role of the intermediary for the most part. I forwarded mails and responded to them as per the instructions of Mr. Feinstein," Helda recounted under the alert stare of Garvey. "I have worked there for one and a half years now."

"Okay," a satisfied prosecutor said. "What about your colleague Sanjeep Raheel? What was her function?"

"To assist Mr. Feinstein as well," Helda replied. "But she dealt mostly with errands—she got him his coffee, bought him this and that, dry cleaner. Mr. Feinstein hired her when I couldn't deal with both errands and the people even though I worked full time. So he hired her part time. And she was suited for the job because she had a rather shy disposition when dealing with people."

"Right," the prosecutor said. "And was there any kind of inappropriate behavior on Mr. Feinstein's part when you worked for him?"

Helda took a deep sigh, exchanged stares with Garvey for a few seconds, then went into a detailed account of her former boss' antics, from his outbursts of anger with Almóndolar, to the way he came on to—and tried to get rid of—"eager" actresses, to using her and Sanjeep as pieces of meat to entice and cajole Garvey's newly hired lawyer into taking care of his dirty business.

Garvey felt crushed by every truthful word Helda uttered, like a torrent of slaps in the face, even though the woman's tone and voice were mild and tempered with emotional pauses. Every bit of information imparted sounded like another knock on the nails being pounded into his coffin. And there was no way to escape.

But that wasn't the worst part. Those accounts by Garvey's secretaries about his indiscretions with them and other aspiring actresses amounted to sexual harassment and sexual battery at most. The most serious account—prosecuted as third-degree sexual assault—the one he expounded on in vivid and ample detail in his online post, was scheduled for a trial two weeks later.

Garvey's fate was in Evelyn's hands. But it seemed settled, as she had already given him his sentence that he had dug his own grave. That phrase had rung so true to him that he felt a chill down his spine the moment he read it. He felt diminished as a result of it, prompting his ego to make himself swear not to ever treat that traitorous woman as anything but an enemy.

But, at the same time, the more reasonable Garvey also knew that getting in her good graces could mean the difference between several years of his life in captivity and him being a free man.

Garvey knew a mild, vanilla text wouldn't elicit a response from the woman he had raped then dumped. So, five days after the first trial, on a gloomy Sunday evening, he swallowed his pride and sent her the following: "I'm gonna die…" hoping to elicit a strong enough feeling of pity, or shock, or at least curiosity to get her to talk to him.

Evelyn was brushing her hair alone in her room, facing the mirror and her thoughts when her phone vibrated. She picked it up and read Garvey's message. Her first reaction was to "pfft…" before immediately putting down her phone, and going back to brushing, to the mirror, and to her thoughts. Except, her thoughts then became dominated by Garvey, by the image of a down-and-out Garvey near a ditch in a dark place in the desert.

"Good!" she said out loud as a reaction to that image, trying to force herself to feel indifferent to that just retribution. But she also couldn't help herself from feeling a pinch of pity and a great deal of curiosity as to how the former big-shot producer was doing exactly.

Evelyn picked up the phone, looked at it, then put it back down.

In the meantime, Garvey gave up staring at his, and thought to himself, "What was I thinking?" for having the credulity to hope for a positive response from the woman he had wronged in so many ways. So he just stood up, and headed for the door to have himself a smoke outside. As the downhearted man put his hand on the doorknob, he heard his phone vibrate. He hurried to his armchair, picked it up, and avidly opened the incoming message.

"You deserve it," the message read. It came from Evelyn.

Garvey was grasped by a sentiment of joy and was holding his mouth from spreading wide open, despite the superficially negative content of the text. "This is a woman just waiting to be convinced," he impishly thought to himself.

The following exchange ensued.

"Why would you say that?" he asked back, hoping to arouse Evelyn and get her invested further in the conversation. "You know that I don't!"

Two minutes passed, and Garvey hadn't received an answer. As he began to lose hope, Evelyn sent, "You're an idiot."

Garvey felt another pinch of joy and hope at her reengagement.

"I am. And I do deserve to be punished, but not with death," he wrote.

"Good thing your just going to prison then!"

Garvey took a minute to think of what to respond to that. She was right, after all. But she was also his only hope for freedom, the only person with the keys to his emancipation.

"What if I got punished in some other way?" he suggested two minutes later.

"What other way?"

"In a way that would make me feel and understand the pain my victims went through."

"Explain??"

"It's a little hard to explain by text. I'd much rather tell it to you in person."

"NO WAYY!" Evelyn objected.

"If you fear I'll do anything to you, I won't, I swear!" Garvey implored. "We'll meet in a public place if you want. I just want you to hear me out for five minutes. If you accept my offer, great. If not, we part ways and you'll never hear of me again. Honest!"

Garvey pressed "Send" with his heart racing, before sending thirty seconds later, "Please!"

A little voice in his head was telling him, "Oh, Garvey. How low have you sunk?" Though, interestingly, that voice remained silent when he had just committed rape. It wasn't the voice of morality—his conscience—but the voice of ego—his pride. And as morally low as forcing oneself on another person was, he was still the dominant party in that dynamic, the powerful one; therefore, he didn't feel his manhood was dented as a result of it. But now, the balance of power was completely reversed as Garvey was sending his obsequious texts; he was the one on his knees this time, and that hurt him like nothing else had.

Yet, while his male ego was being scorched and undermined, he remained hopeful that that steep price he was paying might still lead to a good outcome.

His phone vibrated. "When?" said the text. Garvey smiled and began typing back right away.

The following evening, Garvey was sitting alone in a corner of a diner, sporting sunglasses and a heavy stubble. A woman in a casual burgundy slip dress and sunglasses, too, came in, discreetly looked around, then took a seat at Garvey's table.

"I thought you wouldn't come," Garvey said as he pointed to himself eating. "Fifteen minutes in…"

"That's okay," Evelyn said in a somewhat hushed voice. "I hesitated, to be honest. Even along the way."

"I understand."

The waiter came, and Evelyn just ordered some coffee.

"I missed you," Garvey declared in serious tone as he looked Evelyn in the eye, behind his sunglasses.

"Please…" an incredulous Evelyn said as she looked away.

"What? I do!"

"You have a weird way of treating the people you miss, dropping them like a hot brick," a seemingly disinterested Evelyn reproached.

"I'm very, very sorry," said a contrite Garvey.

"You know what?" she interjected. "I've made my peace with that. Just… Just go ahead and tell me what you came here to say."

Garvey took a dramatic pause looking at the woman in the eye—or rather, in the glasses—and said, "No, you haven't. You're not over it, and you shouldn't be. I deserve to be punished, and you deserve to see me get hurt, to see me getting stripped of the very thing that fuels my engine, my drive, my ambition, of the thing that gets me out of bed…"

"Your penis?"

"No!" spat Garvey with a pretend-indignant look. "Well, actually, yeah. He's been the ultimate motivator. But I'm talking about my money, my wealth. I deserve to lose whatever sum of it you deem just, and that sum will go to you," the man solemnly declared in what sounded like a rehearsed monologue.

Garvey then pulled out a piece of paper and a pen from his jacket, put them both on the table, and told Evelyn to write whatever amount she saw fit, and that it would be hers.

As Evelyn was about to open her mouth to speak, the waiter came with her coffee.

"There you go, ma'am!"

"Thank you."

"You're going to adore the cream on that coffee!" Garvey suggested as he pointed to the cup in a feminine manner.

"Mm-hmm," the waiter concurred with a smile and a knowing raised eyebrow before he turned around and left.

Evelyn just smiled to both men in response as she began to sip from her cup in silence while Garvey was looking at her.

"So what do you think of the cream?" he asked before Evelyn cut him off, and, on a dry tone, asked, "You really think you're going to buy me again? That you're going to buy yourself out of this?!"

"But it's not like last time!" Garvey declared defensively as he was trying to yell and keep quiet at the same time.

"How not?" Evelyn with an expression that was both puzzled and outraged.

Garvey was seeing a side of Evelyn he never thought he would see, as he never knew she had it in her to be this hostile. "Is she doing this just because she can?" he wondered. His most plausible explanation was that she was taking advantage of her current upper hand, and that she was being drunk with power. As she was talking to him and telling him what to do, he gave her a bitter look that said, "Yeah, take advantage of this while you can…"

What didn't occur to Garvey, however, was that the woman may have been genuinely aggrieved, and wasn't just putting the man down as part of an power trip. But whatever was on her mind, Garvey knew he had to convince her and convince her fast, as years of potential freedom—or captivity—were in her hands.

"Because the sum is bigger!" Garvey gushed while gesticulating with his hands before realizing he was being too passionate and toned it down. "The sum would be much bigger, whatever you'd want it to be. I just want you to leave me half a million, and you can have whatever you want from the rest!"

"What's all the rest?" Evelyn asked with the same suspicious countenance.

Garvey grabbed the pen, wrote a number on the piece of paper, and slid it to Evelyn.

Evelyn read it, and opened her eyes in disbelief or excitement. The social-climbing, aspiring actress in her wanted to scream, "Yes!" right away. But she bit her tongue, and instead asked cool-headedly:

"Would that go to me?"

"Yes," a more laid-back Garvey casually answered with the beginning of a grin on his face.

"And what would I have to do for that, in exchange?" the woman asked, still keeping her cool.

Garvey's answer was rendered in one breath: "Tell the jury that the forum account was wildly exaggerated, and that you did somehow give me consent before I roughed you up."

Evelyn slightly raised her head as if she was about to say, "Okay," then stared at that very tempting piece of paper again. She remained silent while Garvey was awaiting a response, but Evelyn couldn't give him more than flustered half-answers. So Garvey cut it short:

"Tell you what," he suggested. "You spend the next 24 hours thinking it through. And we'll meet back here tomorrow, same place, same time, where you'll give me your answer. Sounds good?"

"I can do that," a calmer and more thoughtful Evelyn said.

Garvey smiled approvingly at the woman, lit up his cigarette, and gently asked her to finish her creamed coffee. Evelyn chuckled as a result of this, as it reminded her of her early intimate moments with the man who was always trying to show who's boss. The roles felt reversed all of a sudden, and the man who was almost begging her a moment ago seemed to be the one calling the shots, or at least, trying to.

However, Evelyn got a mental grip and promised herself not to get swayed by his ways anymore, or by the feelings he aroused in her. She just finished her coffee, while Garvey was casually drawing puffs from his smoke and looking out the window pensively.

When the two finished, he stood up, paid for both, and accompanied her out the door with his hand behind her back.

"How did you get here?" he asked.

"Uh, a cab."

Garvey called the woman a cab, and when it stopped, he warmly looked at her and said, "So, tomorrow, same time?" Evelyn responded with a couple of nods while trying not to show the same warmth back.

As she sat in the cab, she just stared off into the distance wondering how on Earth did a meeting that was supposed to be no more than a matter-of-fact transaction ended with such warmth and intimacy. The woman feared she had made her decision the moment Garvey held her by the back, walked her to the cab, and put her in one, with all the resulting fuzziness surrounding that moment.

"No!" Evelyn snapped out loud, leading the taxi driver to take a wary glance at her in the rearview mirror, before she pulled herself together and finished her train of thought in silence.

Evelyn spent her entire way back home ruminating about the conversation she had just had with Garvey. A conversation that was poor in words, but abundant in meaning and emotion. She got out of it more obsessed about the man that caused her so much harm, and, at the same time, felt guilty about that obsession, because she knew the man didn't deserve it.

The next day at the same time, Garvey was seated at the same table with the same sunglasses.

Evelyn came in, this time in a darker dress, taking slow steps towards Garvey, her apprehensive stare hidden behind her own sunglasses, while

Garvey's more libidinous leer onto Evelyn's gait, hips, and legs was hidden behind his.

Evelyn sat down, and Garvey said, "Hi" with a measured smile.

"Hi," Evelyn greeted back.

They both looked at each other in silence for a few seconds, then Garvey asked:

"So, did you settle on a punishment?"

"I did."

"Cool," Garvey said as coolly as he could. "And, uh, is it monetary in nature like we agreed, or is it about that eye-for-eye thing you kept insisting on?"

"Both."

"Right…" he said apprehensively while bobbing his head. "Care to develop on that?"

"Listen, I'm not going to take all that money," Evelyn announced; "just half of it… If you're still okay with settling things with it?"

"I am," Garvey swiftly confirmed.

"Right. So I'll take half of that…"

"And the other half? How am I gonna pay it?"

Evelyn stared at an impatient Garvey, and took a moment to take a deep breath, then asked, "Can you drive me somewhere?"

"Is that part of the punishment?" a puzzled Garvey asked.

"Yes."

"Sure, I can drive!" he enthused, seemingly relieved.

A twenty-minute drive followed, and the "couple" was in Chesterfield Square, where they found themselves in a near-desolate midst of South Central Los Angeles with nothing but shabby-looking bungalows and a few stray dogs sprawling about.

Garvey looked around with a perplexed look in his face, wondering why would Evelyn want to be dropped in that God-forsaken place.

"Do you have some kind of family here or something?" he asked.

"No," she answered, "I just came to see someone real quick. Park near that trailer, please."

"What kind of someone?" Garvey asked while putting his signature "grossed-out" look on his face, with his mouth and nostrils a little open.

"Hold on," said a distracted Evelyn while typing on her phone.

"What the hell is going on?!" a restive Garvey asked more insistently.

Evelyn dismissively told him that she was indeed waiting for family, for her brother, and that she wanted to give him something.

A disheveled, rough-looking black man in a white wifebeater and a thick chain came out of the trailer, walked up to Evelyn's side of the car and offhandedly asked her, "So are we doing this or what?"

Evelyn gave quick, nervous nods to the man and asked him to give them one minute. She then turned to a confused Garvey and confided to him that there was something she had always wanted to do, but was too afraid to ever do it by herself.

"What's that?" Garvey asked.

"I always wanted to try, uhm, heroin?" Evelyn sheepishly replied.

"What?!"

"Please, keep it down!"

"Why the fuck would you do that?!" an aroused Garvey spat.

"Because... Haven't you ever wanted to do something wild?" she entreated. Garvey turned his head and rolled his eyes in disapproval, and Evelyn continued, "Come on! You just assist me! I don't want to be around those methheads alone!"

Garvey sighed, remained silent for a few seconds, then, more calmly, asked, "Why me?"

"Because that's your other half of the punishment," she answered. "That's how you compensate me. And also because I know you won't report me because, well, you know why."

Garvey just stared at Evelyn for a little while, mouth a little open with some incredulity. Once again, he was confounded that a woman who, more often than not, erred on the passive side in behavior and eager to please could be having such vigor in her.

"Okay," Garvey acquiesced in a quieter, more resigned voice.

Garvey and Evelyn followed the young man—Khalil—into the trailer. On their way, Khalil took Evelyn aside to have a talk before they went in. Garvey tried to eavesdrop, but didn't catch much. As the disgraced producer gave a quick glance to them, though, he saw Evelyn discretely slip a bundle of money to Khalil who put it in his pocket.

"Heroin's getting pretty expensive these days," Garvey thought to himself, before turning around, landing a couple of knocks on the door, then opening it and entering.

Inside the trailer, Garvey saw two other, similarly disheveled young men, another black one, and a white one smoking a joint, both of them absent-mindedly facing the TV.

"Hi," Garvey greeted.

"Hey," one of the men replied unenthusiastically, barely acknowledging Garvey.

"So I see you started without us," Garvey said to the man with the joint with a nervous smile, as he tried to make conversation.

Before the pothead completely processed what Garvey said and looked at him, Khalil and Evelyn entered and brought with them fresh down-to-business energy to the room. Garvey turned to them, and started rubbing his hands, all excited at the thought of getting high with Evelyn and the guys. So he just kept making small talk while Khalil and Mike were intently exchanging stares.

"Oh, is that the BBC you're watching?" Garvey cheerfully asked as he pointed to the news on television, while a serious-looking Mike was standing right behind him.

"No," Mike said. "Here's the BBC…"

Shouts of Garvey began to be heard from outside the trailer, as he was telling the men to let go of him, and Khalil telling his homies to hold the large man down tight, and then to unbuckle his pants. Garvey started screaming his lungs out, telling the men to get off of him. The trailer began to shake, and Garvey's screams started to be muddled with sobs and groans, sometimes loud, sometimes hushed, with the trailer rocking, on and off, hard then slow, then hard. It all went on for some ten minutes, during which the middle-aged former mogul wouldn't stop struggling, certainly verbally, and most likely physically as well, going by the movements of the dwelling as well as the bangs against floor and walls inside it.

Five minutes into the show, an inexpressive Evelyn came out. She took Garvey's car, drove herself to his house, and took a cab from there to hers.

All she did along the way was look vacantly into the driver's seat in front of her. When the cab was nearing her home, Evelyn finally showed some emotion: she cracked a slight, satisfied smile. She paid and thanked the driver, then went home and peacefully slept within the hour.

* * * *

The second trial came, and it was Evelyn's turn to testify.

As the woman went up to the stand, Garvey's heart was racing, and when she briefly looked at him, he gave her the look of a puppy dug who was also trying to be threatening, a look that said, "Please! Don't you betray me!" while most of the women in attendance, as well as the entire prosecution, looked at her with support and optimism.

Evelyn's lawyer quickly got down to brass tacks with his client.

"Ms. West," he said. "You have entirely read the account that Mr. Feinstein posted on the website *darkdesires.com*. Is that correct?"

"That's correct," Evelyn confirmed.

"And would you say that account accurately describes one of your experiences with the man?" the lawyer asked.

Evelyn sat silent for a while. Garvey was sweating, his bottom still hurting, his pride hurting even more, and his heart stopped beating, all in the midst of silence so heavy in the courtroom that only one fly could be heard. Until Evelyn slowly replied: "I… Not exactly, actually."

Gasps of surprise rippled through the room upon her response. And the most common facial response to Evelyn's was that of shock, not least of which the prosecutor's. The only exception was Garvey's and his lawyer's who let a smidgen of joyful and hopeful expression transpire as a response.

"Excuse me?" her interrogating lawyer reacted.

"Well…" a discomforted Evelyn fumbled under the pressured of the outraged room, before getting a grip and powering through to tell the whole story. "Most of the details are correct," she informed the judge, the jury, and the rest of the attendees. "However, there is one crucial missing element: consent."

"Consent?" her livid lawyer asked, rhetorically.

"Yes. I, uh, I sort of gave him permission to do that to me," Evelyn confessed, amidst a still-gasping courtroom and rising brouhaha.

"Silence! Silence!" the judge ordered as he struck his gavel three times. "Go on, Mr. Bronski."

"Okay..." the lawyer said as he was trying to gather his thoughts. "So, you're saying you gave Mr. Feinstein permission to rape you?"

"Hold on," the judge interjected. "Excuse me. Is this all news to you, Mr. Bronski?"

"The 'consent' part, yes, Your Honor!"

The judge asked Evelyn why she hadn't shared that information earlier. Evelyn responded that she was too ashamed to admit to having willingly asked for rape. "I hope you understand," she implored. "Who asks to be raped?!" She then continued in a solemn tone and an emotional voice: "But I did. I thought it was sexy at the time. But it was just wrong. And I've been ashamed and disgusted with myself ever since. But then I started to feel guilt for Garvey, because he was being punished for something that wasn't entirely his fault. At first, I thought I should just keep it to myself, because the man is guilty for so many things, that I figured he deserved that anyway. But then, I realized he's already being punished for whatever he did, and shouldn't punished for what he did not. And having non-consensual sex with me, that he did not do. I'm sorry."

A stunned silence fell upon the room. Some of the attendees' mouths were literally agape, especially those who were salivating at the prospect of Garvey being put away for a long time.

Garvey was one of the stunned people as well. And while his mouth was slightly open too, it wasn't because of something Evelyn said; that was just his usual default mouth expression. Still, he felt a mixture of joy at what the woman had just said, and of a newfound respect for her. He looked at her with admiration for having kept her end of the bargain despite the public pressure surrounding her long-awaited testimony. Garvey's eyes kept saying, "Thank you" to the aspiring actress and savior, and when Evelyn's crossed his, they seemed to reply, "Don't worry about it." Though, quickly after, Garvey felt that burning sensation on his bottom that reminded him that he earned this exoneration by the sweat of his brow and cheeks.

While Garvey's subconscious was musing, the judge snapped him out of him by addressing the defense, specifically Garvey's lawyer.

"Mr. Aaronsohn," the judge inquired, "were you aware that Mr. Feinstein had acquired consent from Ms. West prior to the intercourse?"

Garvey's lawyer was caught off-guard just as much as his client and the rest of the attendance were. Fortunately for Garvey, thinking on one's feet was Stuart's forte, so he quickly adapted and jumped on that bandwagon, and, with a ceremonious straight face, replied: "We were, Your Honor. We obviously were. However, I didn't believe it was a credible defense, despite the veracity of it. Women typically do not accuse of rape the men they had just given explicit consent to have sex with. And since there was no proof of it—contrary to the actual forced intercourse laid out on the internet post—we elected not to mention it so as to not hurt my client's credibility despite, again, it being true."

Garvey nodded along his lawyer's smooth and eloquent response in agreement while making a knowing face, and the judge's expressions seemed to find Stuart's explanation sensible. The judge then turned to Garvey.

"So, Mr. Feinstein," he asked, "why did you omit such a crucial element of your sexual act with Ms. West from your description of it? Especially knowing the possible legal repercussions."

Garvey looked at his lawyer as if to ask if he should respond, and his lawyer cautiously nodded.

"Well," Garvey said before he paused, trying to find a good response, "I—Well, that's the point: I didn't know there would be legal repercussions at the time. I was just anonymously posting a story on that forum."

Garvey looked again at his lawyer, who gave him an approving quick nod, suggesting he was doing well. So Garvey went on, "Additionally, that forum was about *rape* fantasies and accounts. So there was no point in telling a story about consensual sex, as forceful as the sex was."

The judge's face betrayed intrigue and suspicion as he listened to Garvey and said, "Uh-huh" as if to affirm he was paying close attention. He then asked the defense if it had anything to add, and the disconcerted lawyer said, "No," before going up to the judge and pleading for an adjournment. The judge acquiesced, and a third and final trial was due to be held three weeks henceforth.

During those three weeks, Garvey attempted to contact Evelyn eight times—through phone calls, texts, emails—but she wouldn't respond, except once, to leave him instructions on where to deposit the money, which Garvey did much later on. The man once showed up at a café she was sitting at, and, as she saw him, she prompty stood up, paid her bill, and briskly walked away.

Garvey received the message loud and clear. Though he felt disappointed by Evelyn's reaction, as he just wanted to talk to her one last time before he was locked away. So he just sent her one last text that said, "Thanks for keeping your word. I'll keep mine."

The three weeks passed, and the final trial began. Helda, Roy, Evelyn, and two other women were heard one last time. And each of the defense and prosecution lawyers made one last plea. The jury went in to deliberate, and four hours later, came back. Of the eight counts of sexual battery, Garvey was found guilty of six; on the third-degree sexual assault charge, Garvey was found not guilty. The judge sentenced him to five years imprisonment, and the disgraced producer was hauled off by officers right away.

Some of the women in attendance cried, including Helda, who was in the arms of an almost-as-emotional Roy, while Rita, from the movie club, watched Garvey being escorted with a modest smile on her face. The people there—victims and sympathizers alike—seemed to have mixed feelings about the outcome: While they were glad the man was finally paying for his harassment and overt and covert blackmail of the women around him, they were still hoping for a rape sentence, which could carry up to eight additional years by itself. But the overall mood was still fairly positive on balance, as well as emotional.

Roy's mood was especially positive as he couldn't help but be taken with pride for setting the whole prosecution in motion. And Helda seemed just as proud of him as she laid her head lovingly on his chest.

Conspicuous among the people in that room was Evelyn, who seemed to having been given the cold shoulder by everyone else then, except by an unknown man who came with her, who seemed to be either a boyfriend or family.

In the week that followed, Garvey's production company was taken over by a senior associate named Bob Brock who was voted in by the board, and who introduced strict sexual harassment rules within it. Producers and directors could no longer have closed-door meetings with actors, although they could assist and opine on the casting process if they wished.

As to Garvey, he spent nearly all of his sentence in protective custody, almost completely isolated from humanity. The only people he interacted with were guards and his brother Rob, who was the only person who visited him—twice—throughout the three and a half years he ended up serving.

But besides that, Garvey just spent his days being lonely, reading Victorian novels and people magazines. He practically devoured those magazines. First, it was to read articles about himself—all of them were negative and depressing, but he couldn't help himself. And eventually, he developed a thicker skin towards the criticism, while also, gradually, gaining a newfound interest in the gossip and the lives of celebrities, which made him avidly go through every article of the four people magazines he managed to get brought in every month. And while scouring through some of the raciest photographs in them, Garvey realized these magazines could serve another vital function besides quenching his thirst for juicy dirt on famous people, which was the same function that got him in that cell in the first place, except the only eager actresses around him then were Rosie and her five sisters.

The three and a half years went by, and Garvey was about to be released on probation. He may have preoccupied himself a lot with the celebrities in those magazines, but one he grew more and more obsessed with was Evelyn, who did end up starring in that Moody Alan movie.

Garvey felt that there was no closure between the two of them, too many loose ends he wanted to deal with, and that drove him crazy. Her movie success, the formidable way she dealt with him during their last encounters, and just her having the upper hand in general both fascinated and crushed him. These things undermined his pride particularly, as he was made to feel lesser to her in an undeniable way. The former mogul relied on an aspiring actress for his freedom, kowtowed to her, gave up much of his wealth to her, only for her to turn him into a plaything to be sodomized by a couple of random junkies. That was what the initial gratitude and appreciation towards her court testimony slowly turned into thanks to the endless alone time Garvey had in that cell and to countless hours of rumination.

* * * *

Once out, Garvey knew he needed to do something big to reclaim his manhood over the woman who, for all intents and purposes, had become more of a man than he was. He needed to change that, and to make her respect him again, as he saw it. Thus, a grand, overwhelming gesture was in order.

The moment he settled on a plan of action, on what to do next, he began mumbling, "I am the Lord thy God… will get you out of Egypt" and "swag" to himself. But first station: the jewelry store.

A determined Garvey went to the store on his very first day of freedom. Right upon his return, he grabbed a pen and paper, sat down, and set to writing then memorizing what he wrote by reading it over thirty times. He then washed, and laid his head on a pillow dreamily thinking about what might be awaiting him and Evelyn the next day.

At exactly seven o'clock the next morning, Garvey's eyes opened. He got up, washed, shaved, put on a suit, and left the house on an empty stomach. Destination: Evelyn's.

By 7:45, Garvey was already parked next to the actress' place, waiting. He didn't know whether Evelyn was alone or not, so he kept looking around him until he saw a child passing by. Garvey got out of the car, gently intercepted the boy, and greeted him with a smile.

"Hey," Garvey accosted the boy as casually as he could, "do you happen to know who lives in here?" he said as he pointed to Evelyn's house.

"Uhh, I dunno," the child said. "I live on the other block."

"Right, right…" Garvey acknowledged distractedly. "Hey, do you want to make a hundred bucks for a two-minute job?"

"Uh, yeah!" the boy enthusiastically replied.

"Alright, so you go to that house, you knock on their door, and you sell them some cookies or something," Garvey instructed. "And then you come back here and you tell me who opened that door, and whether you sensed she was home alone or not. Got it?"

"Uhm, yeah… Except I don't have any cookies."

"Right, right. So how about you go to the store and get some?" Garvey proposed. "I'll add twenty bucks to your fee."

"Meh, I don't know."

"Fifty."

The boy paused, then said, "All right."

"Cool," Garvey said. "Alright, so you go get some of that, and I'll be right here in the car."

The boy dropped by his home quickly to get his bike, then rode to the store and came back in less than ten minutes. When he returned, he knocked on Garvey's car window and asked him what to tell the people who open the door.

"Just say you're selling these cookies for your charity for, uh-- for autistic children," Garvey instructed.

The boy nodded and headed to Evelyn's, while Garvey reversed with his car a hundred yards back to comfortably watch without raising suspicions. From Garvey's perspective, the boy knocked, the door opened, and a few words were exchanged with whoever opened, before the door closed again less than a minute later.

The kid came back with his cookies still in hand. Garvey opened the side window, and eagerly asked:

"So?!"

"A woman in a robe opened the door…"

"Like in her thirties, brown hair, kind of pretty?" Garvey impatiently asked.

"Uh, yes," the boy replied. "I asked if she wanted to buy cookies for my charity. She said she wasn't interested, and she wished me good luck."

"Did you see anyone else in that house? Or hear?" the man asked.

"Um, no, I didn't."

"Uh-huh," uttered a pondering Garvey, before snapping out of his thoughts, then reaching to his pocket, and saying, "Alright, there you go!" as he gave the boy his due. "Thanks, kiddo."

The boy thanked Garvey, then pedalled away.

It was 8:20 in the morning. Garvey vacantly stared at the wheel for a few moments, then puffed in apprehension, and brusquely opened the door and got out of the car, heading towards Evelyn's.

Once standing there, he knocked, then moved to the side of the door. Evelyn came back down, looked into the peephole, but couldn't see anyone, so she figured it was the boy again. She opened and, as she saw Garvey Feinstein standing in a suit, she jumped and screamed in fright before reflexively slamming the door shut. Evelyn started to breathe heavily with her hand on her chest.

"What are you doing here?!" the frightened woman asked.

"I just want to talk to you!" Garvey responded.

"Well, I don't!" Evelyn yelled. "Go away! Go away or I'll call the cops and have a restraining order on you!"

An annoyed Garvey joined the yelling and countered, "For crying out loud, woman, the last time I saw you, I got my ass raped by two black thugs, and you're afraid of *me*?!"

Evelyn's first thought was that Garvey came to retaliate for that very thing. This thought had begun haunting her even when the man was still in prison. So when she saw him, it was as if she saw her biggest specter of the last three years was standing right in front of her.

"Why are you here then?" she asked, still behind her carefully-shut door.

"I told you. I just want to talk to you!" Garvey received no response for some ten seconds, so he continued: "Look at me, Evelyn! Seriously, look at me through the hole! Do I look like someone who came here to do you any physical harm?"

Evelyn cautiously approached the peephole, peaked through it, and saw a clean-shaven Garvey dressed to the nines.

"Just give me three minutes!" the man continued. "That's all I ask for. Just open the door, hear me out, and if you don't like what I have to say, then you'll never see me again, and you can even slap a restraining order on me for good measure. Come on."

Evelyn remained silent for a few seconds, then asked, "Why are you dressed like that?"

"You'll understand once your hear me out," Garvey answered.

"Why can't you say what you have to say behind the door," a still-scared Evelyn suggested. "I can hear you just fine."

"Come on!"

"Either that or nothing," Evelyn announced.

Garvey sighed, then said in a calmer tone, "Okay... Alright, alright. So here goes... As you know, in the beginning, our relation started as purely professional. Or so it seemed. You wanted to star in a film—where you did great, by the way—and I had a say in that, and that was that. At least, on the surface. But what you didn't know, before the trial, was that it wasn't a chance you and Ellen were selected and sent to that hotel. Sure, you did a great job on the audition. But that wasn't just it. The truth is, I had my eye on you since the very beginning. Admittedly, it was through the eyes of my assistant. But the fact remains that you were favored not just for your acting skills, but for a personal affinity I had towards you. And that affinity never waned. I may not have always showed it in the best ways and manners. And for that, I'm sorry.

"You know," he continued, "I spent so much time trying to get women, or get better at getting them. But the truth is, I only needed *a* woman—one I'd connect with both emotionally and physically. And that woman would look and be a lot like you.

"And so, in light of all this, what I'm saying is: I want you to be with me. I want you to be mine—and I'm saying this in the most feminist way possible, if you're one of those. I won't say I'll be spending the rest of my life with you, because I don't like making promises I'm not certain of keeping. But I want you to be mine for at least the next few years. I'd take care of you and you'd take care of me, each in our own ways. And while I might be tempted to stray while with you, I'll promise that I won't—not only because I'd consciously contain myself, but because I'd be less tempted to stray to begin with, because I think in every woman I've gone after, I was really looking for you."

Garvey then got on one knee, opened and put forward the small hard box with a ring in it, and asked, "Evelyn West, will you marry me?"

The door opened, and Garvey looked up to a teary-eyed Evelyn.

"Why now?" asked the tearful Evelyn. "Why now?"

"Because I was blind!" Garvey passionately replied, still on one knee. "I was too blind to see that the things I thought I wanted weren't the things I really wanted. I want *you*! Marry me!"

"No," she answered as she was wiping off her tears.

"What?"

"No," she reiterated with a sad face. "I'm not marrying you. Sorry."

Evelyn closed the door, and left Garvey kneeling there with a ring in hand. She headed to the kitchen, where she sat down then burst out in tears.

"Why now?" truly encapsulated everything Evelyn felt about that man at that moment. A part of her still wanted him too, and was still eagerly waiting for his calls and texts. But what had happened in the past four years made her lose both trust and respect for him, seemingly irrevocably so.

It all felt like such a waste to the both of them. Had the man acted just a little more decently and a little less dismissively when they were together, things would had probably not gotten as bad. Could have, would have, should have.

Garvey, on his part, saw things a little differently. He began seeing her again as the woman who caused him to get raped in the most humiliating and traumatizing of ways. To the former producer, it was multiple times worse than what he had done to her. "Contrary to females and gays," his thinking went, "I didn't enjoy any aspect of it. It was just pure pain and humiliation from start to finish." So, for him, her punishment didn't fit his crime. She was also the woman who took much of his hard-earned fortune away. And who then rejected him when he bared himself to her at her doorstep.

The grand, overwhelming gesture didn't pan out. And Garvey felt even more crushed than he was a day before. Subsumed with anger and desperation, he decided to move to Plan B. Plan B was as much of a grand, overwhelming gesture as Plan A was, but not nearly as charming.

In determined steps, Garvey headed to a nearby shop, made some purchases, then came knocking back on Evelyn's door less than thirty minutes later. Evelyn came to open, and looked into the hole:

"What are you doing back here?" she exclaimed. "I said no!"

"I know, I know," Garvey answered diffidently. "I'm not here for that. It's just that I lost the ring somewhere in here," he continued as he looked around him on the ground.

"How?!" Evelyn asked, still behind the door.

"I don't know, I just lost it!" a seemingly confused Garvey answered, still looking down around him. "I was a little pissed, and I closed the box in snap, and I think that's when it fell off!"

Evelyn didn't know how to respond to that, so she just stood there in perplexed silence, until Garvey resumed talking.

"Listen, you don't have to do anything. You don't have to open the door," he told her. "I'm just informing you of what I'm doing here so you don't get weirded out."

"Alright," Evelyn warily replied, still looking at him through the hole.

Garvey resumed his search, and Evelyn discreetly moved to the adjacent window, watching him behind the curtain. Five minutes passed, and Garvey didn't seem to get anywhere. He began twiddling through the soil with his fingers, then looking into flowerpots. That's when, afraid the man was going to mess up her front yard, Evelyn sighed, then cautiously opened the door and got out.

"I'm gonna help you look for it," she said. "But don't get any ideas! Nothing's gonna change. Okay?"

"Absolutely! No problem," Garvey promptly replied as he continued to search through the ground.

"So where do you think you lost it?" Evelyn asked.

"Somewhere around here," Garvey said as he pointed to an area of the ground.

Evelyn was about to search along with him, but then looked at his hands, and asked with a puzzled face, "Are those gloves?"

Garvey seemed a little flustered by the question. "Oh, yeah," he answered with a nervous laugh. "When I realized I lost the ring in your yard, along the way, I thought I should get myself some gloves at the store, you know, to not dirty the hands too much, which would dirty the suit."

"Right," Evelyn said with an equally nervous smile, not knowing what to think of it, before she began looking for the ring with him. "So when did you get that ring? Did you get it just for me?"

Garvey paused, and said, "Uhm" as if he didn't know what to answer. Evelyn then apologized with an awkward chuckle, and said he didn't have to answer that... Until she saw something else on the ground next to Garvey.

"Can I ask just one last question, though?"

"Yeah," Garvey said casually while still scanning the ground.

"Um, what's the duct tape for?"

Garvey froze, then slowly turned to Evelyn, giving her a dead, but resolved look. Evelyn felt fear build up in her stomach again, and didn't know how to react. She just watched Garvey quickly glancing towards her door left ajar, then the empty street and sidewalks around them, only to turn back to her and pounce on her, aggressively grabbing her by the arm and dragging her inside her house with swift, overpowering force, and shutting the door behind them. Evelyn was not only overwhelmed physically, but mentally as well, and barely moved or said anything during the ten seconds in which all of that happened.

A few seconds later, the door opened again, and Garvey walked back with his arm around Evelyn's neck and his hand shutting her mouth. He ducked down with a struggle while still holding the woman, enough to pick the duct tape and get back up. He then pushed her back in the house with sufficient vigor to hear her body bang against the floor.

Garvey cracked a slight grin as he saw the helpless Evelyn on the floor, and, with an air that was both casual and excited, said, "Here we go again..." before entering and shutting the door behind him.

www.ingramcontent.com/pod-product-compliance
Lightning Source LLC
LaVergne TN
LVHW091555060526
838200LV00036B/844